TOTAL
KNOCKOUT

TOTAL
KNOCKOUT

Tale of an Ex-Class President

★ *Taylor Morris* ★

ALADDIN MIX

New York   London   Toronto   Sydney

ALADDIN MIX

Simon & Schuster Children's Publishing Division

1230 Avenue of the Americas, New York, NY 10020

Copyright © 2008 by Taylor Morris

All rights reserved, including the right of reproduction in whole or in part in any form.

ALADDIN PAPERBACKS, ALADDIN MIX, and related logo are registered trademarks of Simon & Schuster, Inc.

Designed by Jessica Sonkin

The text of this book was set in Bembo.

Manufactured in the United States of America

First Aladdin Paperbacks edition September 2008

10 9 8 7 6 5 4 3 2

Library of Congress Control Number 2008929037

ISBN-13: 978-1-4169-3599-5

ISBN-10: 1-4169-3599-1

★ *To the Lathams* ★

ACKNOWLEDGMENTS

Thanks to all the girls in my summer 2007 writing workshop who gave me brilliant advice and tons of encouragement, especially Sarah Deming, who is too smart and caring for words, and Bridie Harrington, who is as sweet as she is talented. Thank you Jeff Holland for the sports advice you gave that was crucial to the story. Finally, thanks once again to my editor Molly McGuire— New York will never be the same without you!

Cooper "Gravy" Nixon just nailed me with a left hook to the shoulder.

It knocked me back a step, but I regained my stance, my pink gloves on either side of my face. I jabbed right, narrowly missing his chin. He returned the punch, but I weaved around it, then went for an uppercut. Cooper dodged that, too, which frustrated me even more. I knew I was on the verge of losing control. We'd been knocking each other pretty steadily for three two-minute rounds, and we were both sweating and breathing heavily. I needed to focus, but I kept thinking about tomorrow, when I'd become president of Angus Junior High for the third year in a row, the first student to ever accomplish such a feat. Future generations of Angus Blue Jays would revere the name Lucia Latham.

That's me, by the way.

I refocused my energy and upped my momentum, finally landing some solid body shots—and maybe even hitting my best friend a little harder than we normally allowed. But how could he blame me? I was all pumped up on the adrenaline of my final year at Angus Junior High and leaving my mark, my *legacy*, on our school. With each jab I saw my student council victory; with each hook I imagined my eighth-grade year a stunning success; with every uppercut, I envisioned my classmates cheering for my victory.

I guess Cooper finally got frustrated at being smacked around—he is, frankly, stronger (although shorter) than me. He usually just dodges my punches or hits at half strength. I guess he'd had enough, because he pulled himself together and starting swinging back, landing one perfectly executed blow to my cheek. It barely hurt, thanks to the massive headgear our parents make us wear (which also protects our faces), but I still knew in those seconds right afterward that I needed a strategy.

"Ow, Coop," I cried, turning my back on him. "Shoot, that really stung." I peeked over my shoulder. We'd been best friends since before we knew any better—you know, that it's taboo or something for boys and girls to be *just friends*. By the time we figured it out, we were over it and thought everyone else should be too. Still, every so often someone decided to be oh-so-original and ask us when the wedding was.

"You okay?" Cooper panted, taking a step toward me.

"Man, you got me good," I said. "Made me bite my tongue. I thought we said not in the face."

"Hey, I'm sorry," he said, resting his paw on my shoulder. "Does it hurt—"

Turning quickly and deftly, I struck a solid punch into Cooper's stomach. "Fooled you!" I pummeled his body as he twisted his torso, trying to block my ferocious punches. With each hit I silently chanted, *win, win, win, win.*

"Cheater! That ain't fair and you know it!" Cooper hollered as he blocked my punches.

"And another one for bad grammar!" I yelled, jabbing him in the side.

"Fine! I give! Stop it!"

Seeing that he'd really had enough—his round cheeks had flushed a darker shade of red—I lowered my pink Everlast gloves (my prized possession) and wiped away the sweat trickling into my eyes with my shoulder. I extended my hands and said, "Good match, Coop."

He eyed me for a moment, sweat rushing down

his own face. Finally, he lightly tapped my gloves back. "Yeah, you, too," he sighed. "Even if you did cheat."

I pulled off my gloves and headgear and wiped my face with a towel that hung from a gray metal folding chair. The breeze from the open garage door of Cooper's house instantly cooled my face. "Sorry about that. I'm just so pumped about the elections. Aren't you?"

Cooper grimaced. He was only running for secretary at my insistence. He knew how much this final year meant to me, and how much I needed him so that I didn't have any opposition on the council. This way, with my two closest friends, Cooper and Melanie, by my side, I wouldn't have any trouble making all the bold changes I had planned for this year—changes that wouldn't just affect our school, but the entire school district. Besides, Copper was only nervous because he had to make a speech today. Even though he was running unopposed, Mrs. Peoria, the student council advisor, said he had to do it. The election rules clearly stated that everyone had to give a speech to showcase their abilities, so there was nothing I could do.

"Well, I'm excited," I continued when Cooper didn't respond. "Starting high school next year will be like moving up in weight class. That means we have to really prepare ourselves for the next challenge. Now's not the time to get soft."

"I guess," Cooper said, obviously not convinced. He wiped his brow with the bottom of his shirt. I looked away from his exposed belly. "I just hope I don't puke before I can get that speech out."

"It's nothing, Coop. I'll be right there beside you the whole time," I assured him. But he didn't look convinced.

The first few moments when I got back from Cooper's were always my favorite part of the morning. Our house was quiet, with everyone still asleep—we boxed at 6:30—and I always thought that maybe today would be the day Dad would announce that after two months, he'd finally found a job. Mom wouldn't have to work until past dinner every night or nag so much, and things could go back to the way they used to be—easy, stress-free, and normal. Your everyday nuclear family.

In those early-morning-light moments, I felt like anything could happen.

But in two months, nothing much seemed to happen at all. Dad had taught me through boxing that being complacent meant imminent defeat. As soon as you stop moving, stop paying attention, that's the moment you get popped.

I put my gear in my bedroom closet, then headed for the shower. I loved the way boxing made me feel, during and especially afterward, when every muscle felt appreciated and worked, and my mind was cleared. I noticed in the last couple of months that I was developing some muscle on my arms and even my back, which I turned to the mirror to check out, flexing to get a better look. I always gave myself a good salt scrubbing, too, with this yummy stuff Mom got me that has eucalyptus and ginger in it. It was my personal reward for a match well done.

After my shower, I dressed in my most respectable outfit for the student council speeches—navy pants and a bright red button-down. I'd assembled the outfit three days ago with special attention to colors. Red means power, strength, and passion, and blue represents trust, loyalty, and confidence—all things anyone would want in their leader. Plus, every politician I've ever seen on TV wore these same colors, especially during important debates. After combing through my short dark hair, inherited from Dad, I was ready.

In the kitchen, I went to the cabinet for my bowl of organic bran flakes with spelt and flax but instead found something called Bran Bites—one of the few signs Mom was cutting back on expenses. Still, I poured a bowl and a glass of generic-looking orange juice (which did not taste as fresh or pulpy as our usual stuff) and sat down to read over my speech even though I had it memorized: *When I am elected student council president, I will fight for your success, because I believe everyone here has the potential to be the best.* Mom walked in, dressed in a turquoise top, slim black skirt, and black heels with a tiny peek-a-boo at the toe, and started the coffee. She was vice president of her company's online division, and Dad used to like introducing her as the Web Master, which he thought was funny but she never seemed to.

"Henry!" She yelled for my ten-year-old brother for about the millionth time before he finally shuffled in, wearing a black T-shirt with a big white peace sign on it. "You got your lunch money, Lucia?"

I used to pack my own lunch—turkey on wheat, apple, tortilla chips, and water—but starting this year I decided to buy my lunch in the cafeteria. I thought it was impor-tant, as president, to show solidarity with the school.

"Got it." I scooped a spoonful of flakes, careful not to let the milk dribble down my chin. "What's up with the cereal and juice?"

"It's the same as your other stuff."

"These Bran Bites taste like cardboard," I mumbled as Henry popped a frozen waffle in the toaster.

"You should skip that caf food," Henry said, "and try my lunch someday. It's probably more nutritious than that garbage they give you at school."

"Like I'd actually eat your Fluffernutter. Don't the older kids make fun of you?" For someone who had skipped the second grade, you'd think he'd know better than to eat something with zero nutritional value. Our parents had always taught us about healthy food and how it nourished our brains and made us smarter. Since Henry and I were both somewhat overachievers, we usually bought it. Still, Henry was just a kid, and I guess some kids like that kind of "food."

"They don't make fun of me. They want to *be* me." He said this with utter seriousness.

"For someone so smart, you sure are—"

"Okay, you two," Mom said, running a manicured hand lightly over the top of her hair. "Lucia, you ready for your big speech today?"

Asking me if I was ready for my final junior high election would be like asking Pretty Boy Floyd if he was ready to fight Oscar de la Hoya—the guy had only been preparing for it his entire career.

And guess how it paid off. Yeah. He won.

But Mom wouldn't understand or appreciate any boxing analogies—that was Dad's department. She didn't exactly like my boxing—she thought it was barbaric enough when Dad did it—so I tried to keep it under the radar, like boxing before she even got up.

So in answer to her question about my being ready for the speech, I simply said, "Ready steady."

Mom tucked Henry's completely nonnutritious sandwich into a Ziploc bag and muttered, "I wonder if your father plans on making an appearance at breakfast this morning."

Henry and I exchanged looks—we knew that when Mom referred to Dad as "your father," it was best to keep our mouths shut.

Mom deposited Henry's lunch next to his toasted waffles. "William!" she screamed, walking back toward their bedroom. "Your daughter has a big speech today. The least you could do is get up and wish her luck."

It wasn't Dad that I minded, or even Mom—it was the two of them together that wore me out. In the morning, you could count on the nagging and defending being heightened—usually because Mom had worked late and didn't get enough sleep, and because lately Dad had a hard time starting his day.

"I'm out of here," I said to Henry, rinsing my dishes in the sink. "You're on your own, kid."

"Take me with you!" he mock-pleaded.

I grabbed my red plaid book bag, which I carried on special occasions when my rolling backpack looked too junky, and looked out the front window for Melanie. We always met on the corner to wait for the bus together. Cooper rode with his mom; their family Mexican restaurant, which they had opened last spring, was on the way to our school. She always offered to take me, too, but being president of my grade all these years, I felt it important to show that I was just like everyone else, and the school bus was good enough for me. Kind of like the cafeteria.

"Hey, girl. You leave yet?" Dad called from the back of the house.

"I gotta go, Dad," I hollered as I opened the front door, carrying my book bag like a briefcase.

"Well, hey. Good luck!" I saw him as I stepped out the door, standing in his boxers, his eyes still bleary from sleep. I waved before slamming the door and running down the street.

It's not that I didn't want to see him. The truth is, it's hard to see my dad like this, and I kept wondering when he was going to snap out of it. He used to run three miles almost every morning before we were even up, and he went to a boxing gym over in Weatherford several nights a week. He convinced Mom that I should learn the basics of boxing when I was eleven, not for violence or a workout, but for the life lessons it offered. She agreed only after he swore I wouldn't spar in the ring with anyone, under any circumstances, but she still insisted I wear headgear and a mouthpiece, which made no sense because I wasn't taking any punches. This past summer he promised to teach me how to work the speed bag, but then he lost his accounting job to some recent college grad, and his gloves have been hanging in the garage ever since.

I waited for Melanie at the corner of my cul-de-sac. I looked at my watch and saw that the bus would be there any second, and still there was no Melanie in sight. I clutched my cell phone, ready to speed-dial her in case she was lingering in front of the TV, unaware of what time it was. My heart quickened as I told myself that she would make it—both to the bus and to school for her speech. Her dad left for work before the school bus came, and if she missed the bus, he'd usually call in sick for her. He'd done it before, and Melanie had missed a fair amount of school last year because of this. I didn't know Melanie before her mom died three years ago, but I figured her dad's nonchalant attitude toward her schooling was the result of suddenly being a single parent to two girls.

Our student-council plan may seem a bit convoluted, but it really wasn't. See, the election rules were changed five years ago, stating that you can't run for vice president anymore, since the time a bunch of kids ran for veep but no one ran for prez. They just wanted the experience without the responsibility. So now you can only run for president and the other offices, and the runner-up to president becomes the v.p. I know this goes against the democratic ideal, but since nobody at our school cares about the council (besides me), I guess it wasn't a big deal.

That said, if Melanie wasn't at school to give her speech, she would be disqualified from running. I would still be president, but my cabinet would be altered for the worse. I didn't even want to think about the time when my sixth-grade vice president, Steven Francis, shot down my campaign to have electronic hand dryers installed in the bathrooms. Now every time I dried my hands with those scratchy brown paper towels, I felt like I was wiping my hands off with dollar bills. It was so totally economically, not to mention environmentally, unsound.

I spotted the bus coming down the street, and just as it began to slow down, I heard Melanie's front door slam and out she came. She carried nothing but a spiral notebook, strolling down her sidewalk as if it were Saturday afternoon and she was going to check the mail.

"Melanie, hurry up!" I yelled. She looked at me and waved, but I pointed anxiously to the approaching bus. She did a little skip, which made me smile, and as the bus doors opened up, she was right there beside me. I led us to a seat near the front, away from Robbie Cordova in the back, who was in our class and prone to making fart noises if I got too close.

As the bus pulled away, I sat back in my seat and let out a deep breath. "Wearing your red hat for luck today?" I asked Melanie of her favorite red beret.

"My *magic* red hat," she corrected, opening her notebook. "Nothing can go wrong today. As long as I finish this history homework. Did you have this worksheet in your class?" she asked, and I shook my head no. "Can I borrow a pen?"

I gave her one of the many pens in my bag and began to relax, realizing that Melanie's sass and verve were just what a new and improved student council needed. I wondered why I hadn't realized that sooner. As she scribbled in answers on a crumpled worksheet, I asked, "Ready for your speech today?"

Melanie slapped her forehead, almost stabbing herself with the pen. "The speech. I forgot the speech."

"Ha-ha," I said. "It won't work today, Mels."

"I'm serious," she said, and when I looked at her, I knew she wasn't joking. "It's on my nightstand. I think," she added, biting her lip.

My heart raced. "Well, but . . . you have it memorized, right?" I had written both her and Cooper's speeches for them—since this whole thing was my idea, I felt I owed it to them to make it as easy and painless as possible.

"It's pretty much memorized." She twisted the ends of her long hair, her skin blemish-free as always. "I looked at it last night during *Conan*." I leaned my head against the window, feeling the blood rush toward my feet. I hadn't planned on this. Why hadn't I brought extra copies of both their speeches with me? What a rookie mistake. "Loosh," Melanie pleaded, "don't worry! I'll give a great speech today. But not too great! The plan is still in place. You'll totally win the presidency. Just don't freak out on me."

"I'm not going to freak out," I said. Because I wasn't—freaking out wasn't my style. Dad had taught me that keeping your composure was as crucial as a strong right uppercut. If you let some outside emotion get to you while in the ring, then all your physical training was for nothing. "The plan is still definitely in place. I'm not worried. Nothing is going to go wrong."

I said this more to convince myself than Melanie, but I thought it was a pretty bad sign that I didn't even believe my own words.

★ ★ ★ ★ ★ **3** ★ ★ ★ ★ ★

For the entire bus ride to school, I recited Melanie's speech with her, reminding her of the most important parts and suggesting she take notes.

"Don't forget, you're going for second place here," I gently reminded her. "Don't go too crazy, but act like you at least care."

"You think I should spice it up a bit?" Melanie asked, touching her pen to her chin as the bus rumbled toward school. "Like, say something about how much homework blows?"

"No, that's my line. Look, write this down: 'I promise to take this position as seriously as our volleyball team, who were last year's city champs.' Make an exclamation point at the end."

By the time we got to school I felt a little bit better. What I didn't like was that, once she got up on that stage, there was nothing I could do to help her—or myself.

"Oh, hey. Did I tell you?" she said just before we parted for first period. "I'm thinking about trying out for volleyball."

Melanie loved finding new, interesting ways to fill up her time, and she had a closet floor full of abandoned passions to prove it. Most recently it was scrapbooking. She got so excited about putting all her pictures into really cool books, especially shots of her mom. Her dad gave her the money to buy all the stuff, which isn't cheap, but it took a long time to do even one page, and she shoved the supplies in her closet, promising to get back to it soon. Last time I looked, the scrapbooking stuff lay next to her BeDazzler kit, which she had started last winter and given up on before the spring, along with crocheting and the blog she kept for about three weeks. I often thought about joining her in some of her new projects, like the singing lessons she did for a few weeks last fall. I worried, though, that it would take away from boxing and school.

After first period, I hustled to my locker so I could get to the auditorium early for the student council assembly, which happened during second-period homeroom.

I wanted plenty of time to settle in and get focused. As I dumped my books and took out my speech, I searched the halls for Melanie. Instead I saw Nicole Jeffries practically dragging her Tevas-clad feet down the hall, headed straight for me. Nicole had been the school's sleuth reporter since sixth grade, and she was dang good at what she did. We didn't hang out together, but I'd always liked her—she had the same drive and ambition for reporting that I had for politics. And just like I knew that I would one day be Speaker of the House, Nicole would no doubt end up writing for the *New York Times* someday.

"Lucia, hey." Nicole always seemed unfazed and slightly bored, probably because she wanted to keep impartial and focused about the stories she embarked upon. She'd interviewed me several times for various president-type things and always kept the same demeanor. "So, can we schedule an interview after the election tomorrow? Since you're basically running unopposed, it won't be a shock when you win, but I'd like to get your statement on what it's like to be the only Blue Jay to be president all three years."

"Yeah, sure," I said, excited about my future accomplishment. "Wanna talk at lunch tomorrow?"

"Sounds good," she said, writing this down in her lavender notebook. "Good luck at assembly."

In the auditorium, students filed in, screaming, laughing, pushing, and generally acting as if they were getting in line to appear on the next MTV reality series. Girls were talking and texting at the same time, and some guys were playing keep-away with a science book that belonged to some sixth grader.

"Lucia! Hey! Lucia!"

Max Rowe, one of Cooper's friends, was waving wildly at me as if he were flagging down a rescue plane. I smiled and waved back, if only to settle him down.

"Good luck!" he called.

"Hey, Lucia!" called a football guy who didn't like Cooper for absolutely no reason that I could even fathom. There was nothing controversial or offensive about Coop. "What are you going to make us do this year? Wear uniforms?"

I politely ignored him.

On TV shows and movies they act like if you're student council president you're automatically popular, but not at Angus. Some people respected the student council—like the Fun-Guys, a biology group dedicated to all things fungus—but most people thought we were a big joke, the nerds who never got spring break extended, free school supplies for everyone, or Taco Bell served in the caf. I don't think most people understand what it took to make changes that were both popular and meaningful. Still, I took my job seriously and did the best I could for each and every student. I really did.

When I got backstage, the first thing I saw was Cooper leaning his forehead against the wall.

"Hey, you okay?" I asked. I poked his shoulder to get his attention.

"I'm not exaggerating," he said, panting, his skin pale. "The Shredded Sugar Shots from breakfast are about to make a comeback."

"Jeez, Cooper. You really should eat a better breakfast. No wonder you're about to pass out, eating that kind of—"

"Lucia! Seriously!" he snapped—pretty loudly for someone who was allegedly on the verge of collapse.

"Take deep breaths, Coop. Relax. This will all be over in five minutes. Okay?" He nodded, his eyes closed. "I'll be right back, okay? I'm going to go look for Melanie."

I was actually going to ask, beg if I had to, Mrs. Peoria if she would let Cooper go first, even if the speeches were supposed to start with the treasurers. I couldn't let him hang in agony like that, especially since he was only doing it for me.

"I don't care," Mrs. Peoria said, barely looking at me when I asked. She always had brown circles under her eyes, making her look sleep deprived. I wondered what might keep her up all night, stressed and worried. "Do what you want, Lucia." Anyone could see she hated being the student council adviser. I think someone forced her to do it because she's the social studies teacher, which I guess meant she knew the most about student government stuff.

When I got back to Cooper, he was sitting on the floor, his back to the wall and his legs splayed out in front of him. Color had returned to his cheeks, but his eyes stayed closed. "Have you seen Melanie?" I asked. He rolled his head from side to side. "It's going to be fine, Coop. You'll do great!" He moaned in response.

I looked around at the other candidates for eighth-grade council. There was Jared Hensley, who was friends with Robbie Cordova from the bus; Jared was an arrogant guy who thought he was smarter, more popular, and better looking than he actually was. Also running was a mousy girl named Lily Schmidt, who was extremely shy and socially awkward—rumor had it that running for student council was part of a plan devised by her therapist to help her break out of her shell.

"Okay, children! Let's get lined up!" Mrs. Peoria clapped. I have a theory she called us "children" just to spite us. How would she feel if I called her "old lady"?

Melanie was still nowhere in sight, but I tried to concentrate on my speech instead of worrying about her. Onstage, I sat in my chair with my ankles crossed. I remembered the first year I went through the elections and how nervous I'd been. But after the speech, I had felt such an overwhelming sense of accomplishment from giving my first political speech that from that moment on, I was hooked. I only wanted to get better as a politician. And over the last two years, I think I have. I've learned a lot—like how it's important to have friendly people on your council.

When Mrs. Peoria called Cooper's name, the crowd gave him an enthusiastic cheer, making me beam with pride. Most people—aside from petty jerks—liked Cooper because he was so sweet and got along with most people. As he dragged his feet to the podium like he was about to run suicides, I wondered why today of all days he couldn't tuck in his shirt. His standard uniform was an oversized polo shirt, untucked, with baggy jeans. I looked stage left for Melanie, but there was still no sign of her. I took deep breaths and told myself not to worry.

Opening his crumpled speech—right into the microphone—Cooper read through it so quickly that it was as if Terrell Owens was about to come give him a smack down. If I hadn't written the speech, I wouldn't have been able to understand a bit of it.

"FellowstudentsofAngusJuniorHighIwantyouto knowthatIwillbethebeststudentcouncilsecretarythis schoolhaseverseenIamveryefficientaccurateandorganized andwilltothebestofmyabilitiesupholdallthatmyduties requireandmoreeverystudentofDouglasAAngus JuniorHighcanrestassuredthatwhentranscriptsofour meetingsareneededtheywillbeofutmostaccuracysoplease voteforme. Ugh, Cooper Nixon, for student council secretary. Thank you."

Cooper practically ran back to his seat as the crowd cheered. I clapped along with them, smiling and happy that he'd made it through the worst part; now he could sit back and relax. Which was more than I could say for myself. Where *was* Melanie? I craned my neck for another look into the wings, hoping to spot her. I wondered if something was wrong, and then felt bad for worrying about myself when it was possible that Melanie had sneaked off campus because of a sudden urge for toffee candy, only to be abducted by—

"Lucia Latham!"

I snapped to, seeing Mrs. Peoria staring me down from the podium through lazy wisps of straggly brown hair. I wiped my slightly sweating palms on my pants, composed my face, and walked carefully, deliberately, to the podium. I held my head high like Hillary Clinton always did, no matter how many people hated her guts.

"Students of Angus Junior High," I began, looking out into the crowd. I noticed a low rumbling of conversation and quiet laughing, which Mrs. Peoria seemed oblivious to as she sat rubbing her temples. I spotted Max in the crowd; he was once again waving at me. "Before I begin, can I get a round of applause for our football team, who I know will stomp on those Keller Cougars this Thursday night?" The students perked up, whooping happily. "Good luck, guys. I hear we have a record number of players this year, and I have a feeling this is going to be the best year ever for our fighting Blue Jays!" More hollers, applause, and *We're number one* filled the auditorium. "When I am elected student council president, I will fight for your success, because

I believe everyone here has the potential to be the best. Proven!" I called, raising my arm for emphasis. "I have proven myself to be a strong leader who gets results. Last year, as I'm sure you remember, I spearheaded the petition, signed by one hundred and twenty-seven of you, saying we wanted homework cut down. And what happened? Ms. Jenkins met with the teachers, who united against excessive homework."

That got a round of polite, albeit lethargic, applause. Most people didn't believe the homework had decreased at all. No worries, though, because as I looked out at my people, I willed myself to energize those comatose faces. I wanted them to care as much about the council as I did—or at least to see that we really did do things that mattered. Things for *them*. It was my last year to prove that what I did counted.

I struck my fist as I swore that every classroom would have a recycle bin. I pounded the podium as I vowed the cafeteria would serve more nutritious foods. I could feel my brow dampen as I lamented on the utter lack of an arts program and guaranteed that every student would be given the opportunity to play an instrument if she or he chose to. Okay, so maybe I went off script a little, but I felt so in the moment, yet out of it at the same time, like I was having an out-of-body experience. Words flowed without effort, without thought, without once referring to my speech. My chest rose with each new promise, each new declaration, and when I pointed out into the auditorium filled with students I would spend my final year at Angus with, I heard myself bellow, "If Lucia Latham wins, so do you!"

I thought I'd hear a rousing round of applause. There I was, practically promising to change their lives, and all I saw was a bunch of slack-jawed students staring back at me. I realized Mrs. Peoria was standing beside me, a forced smile on her face. Nudging me aside, she leaned into the microphone and stuttered, "W-well. That was very . . . energizing. Let's give a hand to Miss Lucia Latham, everyone."

It was sparse applause, at best. As I walked back to my seat, I tried to figure out what had just happened. When I saw Cooper's face, I realized I may have been a little overzealous. His eyes were wide, almost frightened, like they were this morning when I popped him a little harder than I should have.

It wasn't until she practically ran onstage from the back, her curls bouncing with each step, that I realized

Melanie had finally arrived. She clutched a plastic bag and her face was flushed.

She mouthed, "It's okay," as she took her seat at the end, dropping the bag onto the floor and adjusting her red beret. When Mrs. Peoria called her to the podium, my stomach cramped up, wondering what was about to happen.

Even though I wrote Melanie's speech and then recited it back to her that morning on the bus and forced her to take notes, once she was up at the podium her actual speech went like this: "Who wants free stuff?" The crowd cheered. "Vote for me and I'll give you free stuff!" And then she reached into her bag and began throwing what I later found out were black-and-white pirate pencil toppers. Students leaped over seats and each other in such pandemonium that Mrs. Peoria and our principal, Ms. Jenkins, finally had to physically restrain Melanie from throwing any more, like a ref stopping a fighter after the bell.

"Enough!" Mrs. Peoria yelled into the microphone as students tumbled on top of each other as if they were fighting for the latest Nintendo Wii game.

I couldn't believe what I was seeing. If there's one thing people like, it's free stuff. I don't even think it matters what it is, just as long as they're getting something for absolutely nothing. Plus, it looked like they were finally having fun. To make matters worse, I knew that Melanie's doing this would make her seem sort of . . . cool. Her social status had dangled on the outer fringes, as many people had been afraid to approach her in the past, since she was the girl whose mom had died. For me to be president, Melanie had to come in second place, but with the pirate pencil toppers, I had a feeling that her social status had just been upped. Which meant the presidency might not be mine anymore.

In the midst of the chaos, I slipped offstage and hid behind one of the musty black curtains, telling myself to relax, to take it easy like Melanie always does. I gulped in deep breaths and tried not to freak. This would be, *had* to be, my best year yet.

4

"Did I ever tell you about the time I kissed my elbow and turned into a girl for a day?"

Cooper had shown up on my doorstep just moments after I got home. When I walked into the house, I'd heard Dad shuffling around in the back, but only yelled, "I'm home!" before settling on the couch with Paddy, which was where I still was when Cooper came over. I hadn't even bothered to look at my homework yet.

On days like this, I found Patchwork Puppy—aka, Paddy—more comforting than a reading assignment. My grandmother made him for me when I was three, out of old scraps of fabric she had lying around her sewing room. He was the shape of an *H* and worked equally well as a small pillow or a type of security blanket—my arm hooked right around his center, between his tail and his head. There was no other stuffed animal in the world like Paddy—he was an absolute original.

"I bet if you kissed your elbow, you'd turn into a boy for a day. You should try it," Cooper continued. I flipped through the channels on the TV, past shows I might normally watch but today didn't care about. "Look, it really wasn't as bad as you think. I mean, it wasn't bad at all. Loosh? You okay?"

"I'm fine," I said. Ever since that stupid assembly, I'd wondered how the student body could ever take me seriously if I went off like a lunatic during my big speech. I reminded myself of that clip of Howard Dean I once saw on YouTube. When Lori Anne Overton, the yearbook photographer, snapped my picture as I cast my vote after the assembly, I smiled as if I had already won. But really, I was worried that everyone thought I was a crazy has-been, and that someone more fun and fresh— like Melanie—might be just the thing to make them really care about what the student council did.

One of the reasons winning in my final year was so important was because of the plaques. Each year, the graduating student council held a fund-raiser for something that the school needed. It varied every year and was dictated to the council by the PTA. Last year's eighth-grade president, Mandy Donath, held a craft fair to raise money for new art supplies. In the art studio there was a plaque that had the year Mandy and her student council graduated and said, *Our new equipment has been generously donated by the student council, Mandy Donath, President.* These plaques go as far back as the 1970s. They left an indelible impression on the school for generations to come.

I wanted my name on one.

The PTA didn't decide what deserved the student council's fund-raising efforts until about a month into the school year. They wanted the money raised by winter break so that whatever it was being used for could actually be utilized during the school year. I didn't know what we'd be raising money for, or how I would conduct my fund-raising (although I had some ideas), but I knew that this final year of council was definitely the most important, in more ways than one.

As I flipped through channels, Cooper continued telling me about the day he turned into a girl and how it made him act super bossy and crave chocolate. I ignored these female clichés. He'd been telling me these silly little lies since we were seven and I lied about ruining his signed Nolan Ryan baseball card.

I know. I'm awful.

It was his birthday, and he'd come down to my house to show off the signed card, which was in pristine condition. I'd heard of Nolan Ryan but didn't know anything other than he was some old baseball player who used to pitch for the Texas Rangers. Cooper was visibly bummed when I barely gave it a once-over, so I started acting interested.

"Here, let me see it." Cooper had handed me the card, watching closely as if I were holding a newborn. "Yeah, that's pretty cool, Coop. I bet this is worth a lot of money."

"He's a living legend," he said proudly.

After a few minutes I put the card on my desk and suggested we watch a movie in the living room. I didn't realize he'd left it behind until the next morning when I spilled orange juice all over it.

The doorbell rang while I was wiping up the sopping mess, and I heard my mom say hi to Cooper. A moment later, he showed up in the doorway.

"Hey, Loosh. I left my . . . what happened?" He looked stricken when he saw his card in the puddle of juice.

"Henry," I cowardly said. I couldn't look Cooper in the eye and see the devastation I'd caused. "He was in here playing even though he's not supposed to, and when I came back from the kitchen I found this."

"My card," Cooper said mournfully, peeling it carefully off my desk.

A couple of days later, Cooper said he was sure Henry felt awful about what had happened and told him it was okay and he wasn't mad. Henry was only four at the time, but he was smart enough to proclaim his innocence. When Cooper confronted me, I felt so ashamed—not just because of the lying, but for blaming it on my little brother. Once Cooper accepted my groveling apology, he began teasing me about my trying to make a blameless child take the fall.

Since then, he's always coming up with extravagant stories to show me how ridiculous I'd been. The first was when he told me his mom was letting him change his middle name to Gravy because he loved the stuff so much. I dared him to drink it from the gravy boat one night when I had dinner at his place, and he did—half the boat, which is a lot of gravy. He'd long since forgiven me, but he still loved making up stories.

"So when you were a girl," I asked Cooper, still flipping through channels, "did you wear a dress and play with dolls?"

"About as much as you ever did," he said.

I smiled and tossed the remote control aside and said, "Know what I want to do? Go down to your house and box."

I was the one who got Cooper into boxing. Actually, I don't know if he's really into it or if he does it just for me. Either way, he never turns down a fight with me, and his form has gotten really good over the last year. I taught Coop everything he knows about boxing, just like my dad taught me.

Dad was the Golden Gloves Junior Middleweight champion of North Texas for two straight years. This was way before I was born, even before he married Mom. Those fighting days, he says, were the best of his life. And I believe him, too. When Dad talked about his days in Teddy KO's Gym in Arlington, his eyes lit up with a fiery intensity that made you want to listen.

He'd tell about the dingy gym that he loved so much—the smells of sweat, blood, and raw determination; the sounds of leather on flesh, of grunting, of jump ropes smacking the cement floors. He talked about fights when he literally didn't think he could raise his arm for one more punch but willed himself to keep going until he got that knockout. "Just goes to show," he'd say, "that there's always a little more in you than you think."

Dad was boxing when he met Mom. She fell for the whole brute-contender thing, but when they got serious, Dad realized he needed a real job. He got his CPA license, they got married, and he kept fighting bouts. But when Mom got pregnant with me, she told him she was worried that it was too dangerous, so he quit competing. He kept boxing in the evenings at the gym and did some friendly sparring, too. Once I came home from the hospital, Mom said it wasn't fair that he got to go out four nights a week to the gym while she stayed home with me. So Dad cut it to just one night a week and early Sunday mornings. That worked for a long time—basically until this summer, when Dad got canned from his job and stopped doing pretty much anything. I guess you could say he'd given up the fight.

The afternoon of the election, as we boxed in Cooper's garage even though we were still pretty beat from that morning, I kept seeing Melanie flinging those pirate pencil toppers into the crowd. Every time I pictured the faces of the ecstatic, rejuvenated students grabbing that loot, I threw my upper body into hooks and jabs. And maybe I hit Cooper a little harder than we normally allowed, but he didn't say anything. He didn't even call quit when I could see he was dying for a break, sweating and panting, his face as red as his gloves. I needed a break too, but I think I was too jacked on adrenaline to stop—my body simply kept going.

When our automatic buzzer signaled the end of an intense second round, I looked at Cooper panting in his corner of the garage and asked, "You want to stop, Gravy?"

"No," he said. "Looks like you need it."

"I'll slow it down."

He nodded, and when the buzzer signaled the end of the thirty-second break, he put his gloves back up to his face and blocked my punches.

When I got back home, I put my boxing bag in my closet and hit the shower, taking my time like I usually did. I was running low on my eucalyptus-and-ginger body scrub and needed to ask Mom for more. When I got out I put on some stretchy pants and a T-shirt. I felt better about the elections—Cooper assured me that I would still win and asked for the millionth time if I was mad at Melanie. "Mad about what?" I'd kept asking as visions of pirates swirled in my head.

I was trying to do some homework but really just obsessing about what happened at the assembly, when Melanie called on my cell. I hesitated, and felt horrible even as I hit the reject button.

I went in search of life in our house. Henry wasn't in his room, although his backpack sat next to his desk, and Mom's car still wasn't in the driveway, even though it was almost seven o'clock.

Back in the office, I found Dad at the computer. He wore an undershirt and old running shorts, no shoes. He looked over the monitor at me and smiled. "Hey, honey. You have fun at the Nixons'?"

I nodded. I wondered if he'd left home all day, and if he'd gone back to bed after we'd all left the house that morning. I wondered if he was going to make dinner, or if Henry and I would just get something on our own, like we were doing more and more often these days.

"What are you working on?" I asked, trying to be hopeful. I'm not sure any of us knew what he did all day—what he'd been doing for two months—but I still held out hope that even if he'd given up the thing he loved most, meaning boxing, he hadn't given up the thing he *needed* most, meaning a job.

Dad smiled at me in his don't-rat-me-out kind of

way and turned the monitor toward me. He'd been playing solitaire.

"Oh," I said, overcome with disappointment. Usually when he gave me that look it was because he'd had an actual fight at the gym instead of just working out. "Where's Henry?"

"At Simon's, working on a science project."

"When's Mom coming home?"

He leaned back in his chair. "Probably in an hour or so. Want to help me get dinner started?"

"I have homework," I said, even though I was starving and intended to sneak into the kitchen for some peanut butter and apple slices. He hadn't even asked about the assembly. Two years ago, on the morning of my first assembly speech, he'd gotten up early and made me whole wheat pancakes for good luck.

"Well, y'all holler if you need anything. Okay, honey?"

He smiled at me, that smile that used to tell me there was nothing to worry about.

I went back to my room, shut the door, and clutched Paddy.

★★★★★ 5 ★★★★★

The next morning I waited for Melanie at the usual corner. Butterflies raced through my stomach, wondering how the elections would play out. If I was honest with myself, I knew that, way deep down, I would probably still win. But with Melanie's exciting performance, and the general lack of enthusiasm for the council in general, I had some major doubts.

At least Melanie was treating the day the same as always—she trotted out of her house just as the school bus pulled up, wearing a brown men's derby with a small pink flower she had plucked from her yard tucked into the band. Seeing her look so pretty, fresh, and relaxed put a smile on my face. As she took her breezy time walking to the bus, I realized how immature I'd been last night by screening her call.

"So," Melanie began, "you okay about yesterday?"

We sat in our usual seat near the front. "I tried to call you last night. Did you get my message?" I could tell she was eyeing me closely, trying to gauge my mood. When I didn't get Ms. Jenkins's approval last year to eliminate home ec in lieu of sex ed, I got so red-faced angry that Melanie literally backed out of my room and walked a path around me for two days.

Before I could answer Melanie, something pelted me in the back of the head. We turned around to see Robbie Cordova with the most blatantly innocent look on his face as he concentrated on staring out the window. Melanie reached under the seat, and when she opened up her palm, she asked, "Oh, hey. Did you get one?"

The dreaded pirate pencil topper.

Melanie and I looked at each other, and I could feel my pulse quicken. She readjusted her derby hat, then turned back to Robbie and said, "Why do you even have one of these? It's not like you know how to write." But he only howled with laughter.

"Anyway." Melanie sighed. "I totally thought Mrs. P was going to start foaming at the mouth or something at the assembly."

As she went on to tell me how she'd gotten the freebies (her dad, a marketing guy, had them left over from an event and Melanie called his secretary to bring them in), I tried to think of her as I hadn't yesterday—as an opponent. I knew that, just like in boxing, you should never underestimate your opponent. I started to wonder if I had underestimated Melanie. It's not like I was her only friend. There were a couple of girls she hung out with at least as much as me. I guess I had wanted to think of her as my comrade in arms, but the truth was, Melanie worked in her own world, one that was fun and friendly and open. I wondered, not for the first time, if the students could accept me for being so serious all the time. But just like Melanie's breezy attitude made her who she was, my studious ways made me who I was.

At least, that's what my mom always said.

I didn't want to be mad at Melanie because she had only done what I asked—more or less. I knew that I was a little jealous—no, *envious*—of her ability to be spontaneous and laugh things off. I figured it was something she'd worked pretty hard to learn to do since her mom passed away.

Melanie's mom died when we were in fourth grade, before she and I became friends. Cooper and I had never known anyone who died, or anyone who *knew* anyone who'd died. We wanted to stare at Melanie in the halls and in class to see what a person who had lost a parent looked like. Would she break down and cry at any moment? Was she bitter, and would she soon turn into a bad girl? Could you tell just by looking at her that she didn't have a mom anymore? The truth was, there weren't any signs written on her face. She was out of school for a week and came back the next Monday. Maybe we did all stare at her too much, because by Wednesday she was gone again for the rest of the week. After that she came back again, wearing a pink camouflage military hat pulled low over her eyes, but she was smiling. I even saw her laughing between classes with her sister, Beverly.

I didn't become friends with her until last year, even though we lived so close to each other. Melanie and her sister, Beverly, who was two years older, were always close, but after their mom died, they became inseparable. No one at our school could get through their force field. They walked to class together and sat alone together at lunch. Last year, though, Beverly moved on to high school, leaving Melanie behind. Melanie had other friends, like Rose Andreas, who was in my homeroom (along with Robbie Cordova), but I wasn't really friends with them. Rose didn't ride the bus, and with Beverly in high school, Mel sat alone. One morning I asked if she wanted to sit with me. I wouldn't have thought we'd become such good friends—Melanie is the type of girl who always says yes, whereas I liked to think of the pros and cons of things, but I think that her willingness is part of what I liked about her. Still do, actually.

We were almost at school when I took a deep breath and asked her the question that'd been nagging me. "Hey, Mel? Do you want to be president?"

For a moment I thought she was going to say yes— something about the way she darted her eyes at me. But she said, "God, no! It seems totally boring. No offense," she added. "Besides, I feel like I'm already so swamped with school that I wouldn't have time anyway."

"Well, do you want to be vice president?" I didn't want her to want what I wanted, but I wanted her to at least want what she wanted—even if I did sort of orchestrate the whole thing. If that makes sense.

"Oh, sure," she said. "Being the veep sounds like fun. Plus there's no, like, real responsibilities, right?"

"There are some responsibilities," I said. "It's not a total cake thing."

She waved her hand and said, "It'll be fun."

As the bus pulled into school, I had a sinking feeling

that maybe, just maybe, things weren't going to turn out the way I'd planned.

In first-period algebra, everyone seemed like they were having a grand ol' time working out their quadratic equations—probably because everyone's pencils were topped with a pirate. Even Lily Schmidt, who had apparently gained some confidence from her six-word speech yesterday ("I'm Lily Schmidt. Vote for me."), turned around and told me, "I nabbed an extra if you want one."

In homeroom, I thought about how I should react, both if I won and if I didn't. Gracious, either way. I figured I would smile if I didn't win, maybe even shrug in a sort of, *What can you do?* kind of way. And if I won, maybe I should put my hand to my chest, bow my head, and mouth, *Thank you.*

When our principal finally came on the speaker, my heart pounded—I was more nervous than I thought I would be. I realized at that moment that I did care whether or not I won—a lot. I wanted to win. I had to win. Who was I if I didn't win?

"Attention all Blue Jays," Ms. Jenkins began. "I have the student council election results I know you've all been waiting for." I looked around the room and saw

Rose Andreas giggle and roll her eyes. I wondered what Melanie had said to her about running for vice president, and if maybe Rose told her she was wasting her time.

"Let me just begin by saying that this year's election was the closest presidential election in the entire history of our student council. I believe that *all* our candidates deserve our thanks for giving us such a rousing election this year." I kept my face forward and tried to hold what I thought was a pleasant, slightly curious expression on my face.

"Let's not delay another moment," Ms. Jenkins continued. "Here are this year's student council officers! Beginning with treasurer—Jared Hensley!"

"Ah, yeah." Robbie laughed. "He's going to party away the money."

"Student council secretary belongs to . . ." Ms. Jenkins paused for effect, like she was naming the top ten in the Miss America pageant. "Cooper Nixon!"

I wanted to burst out clapping for my best friend, but managed to hold back. I knew people would vote for Coop, and I was so excited to get to work with him on council. This was going to be the best year yet. *If* I won, I had to remind myself.

"Now, as you all know, we had very spirited speeches this year, and the race for the presidency was close. Both Lucia Latham and Melanie O'Hare deserve kudos for their efforts. This race was close. But this year's student council presidency goes to . . ." Ms. Jenkins paused again for dramatic effect. *Keep a pleasant face*, I told myself. *Act gracious, no matter what.* ". . . Lucia Latham!"

I pumped my arm and cheered, "Yes!"

As the others in my class openly laughed at me, I pulled myself together and thought, *So much for gracious.*

Leaving homeroom I secretly wanted to walk the halls to throngs of "Congratulations, Lucia!" and "It's great to have you back for a third year!" Or something. I don't know why—it'd never happened in the past. I guess I hoped that maybe this year would be different. I had made history and thought that was worth something.

Like a true best friend, Cooper was the first to congratulate me. He high-fived me in the hall when I passed him walking with Max, who yelled, "Way to go, Prez!" I didn't want to think he said that just because he was with Cooper, but it made me smile anyway.

Nicole Jeffries was the only other person at school who said anything to me, and that's just because of the interview.

"So, same time tomorrow morning, Madam President?"

"Yeah, I guess."

I felt very strange. Like I was completely unsatisfied, which didn't make sense because I had gotten exactly what I wanted. I started to wonder what would make me happy, and the only thing I could come up with was a little bit of recognition. I mean, if they took away the student council tomorrow, not one person, besides me, would care. But what everyone didn't know was how helpful the council could be. Like with the homework thing, which I believed had been cut down a bit.

"Hey, you okay?" Cooper asked after school before I got on the bus. I could see his mom's new silver Lexus waiting to take him home. When I told Cooper I was fine, he asked, "You didn't think you wouldn't win, did you?"

I shook my head, no. The truth was, I'd been rattled by Melanie's ability to engage the crowd—the very thing I never could do. I know what she did was a little less . . . *refined* than the speech I gave, but I felt like I was looking at her more closely for the secret to getting people to care about what I did.

And when I climbed onto the bus, Melanie was already there, saving me a seat, her pink flower slightly wilted but still bright and cheerful.

"You did it!" she cheered, grasping my hand. "Not like everyone didn't know you would, but . . . yay!"

I was happy and knew I had to stop being so weird about the whole thing. I squeezed Melanie's hand back and said, "I won!"

She clapped her hands and hooted, and I felt all my anxiety go away.

"Look! It's President I Hate Fun," Robbie called from the back of the bus—and back came the anxiety.

"Shut up, jerk!" Mel snapped. Turning back to me as if nothing had happened, she said, "Want to go to the mall with me later? Beverly is meeting up with some guy she met and I need new shoes for volleyball try-outs. Oh, did I tell you? I'm trying out next week."

I was about to ask her if she thought volleyball would interfere with student council but decided not to. One, because I didn't want to be a nag like my mom, but also because I secretly wondered if she'd stick with volleyball long enough to even be on the team. I felt bad for thinking that, especially after what she'd done for me. Instead, I told her I had a lot of homework and just wanted to stay at home.

★

The day that I won my third junior-high presidential election, sealing my status as a history maker at Angus, I came home to find the house completely and utterly empty. I'm not saying that because I felt sorry for myself, but it was odd. Mom was always working; Dad was always *not* working; and Henry had exactly one friend, whose house he went to only occasionally.

I went to my room and pulled my school stuff out of my bag and sat at my desk. I turned on my computer and arranged everything just so, like I normally do before getting down to work. I repositioned my framed, autographed picture of Nancy Pelosi, which Cooper had gotten me for my birthday, took out my notebook, and got to work on Important Project Number 1 for my final year at Angus. I hadn't told anyone about it, not even Cooper. Not that I thought he'd tell anyone, or that he'd think it was stupid or impossible or something. It's just that I felt that the more control I had over the projects, the better their chances of success.

I got so involved in my research that I didn't realize Mom and Dad were home until I heard them arguing in the kitchen. I also realized I was starving, but before I went to investigate, I wanted to see if Henry was in his room, away from the fighting. They'd been fighting a lot since Dad got laid off. I'd heard Mom tell him more than once that he hadn't even tried to save his job. Dad said that maybe losing it was a blessing, which only made Mom angrier.

I knew all the yelling had to be scary to Henry; it was scary to me. And even though he's practically a boy genius, skipping second grade and now making all *A*s in his advanced classes, Henry was still a kid, even if he was totally precocious.

His bedroom door was mostly shut; I nudged it open. Inside, I found him lying on his stomach on his bed, reading a book. I could hear my mom telling my dad in a very loud voice that he could at least clean the kitchen, to which he said, "I'm going to!"

"You okay?" I asked my brother.

"Fine," he muttered. "I'm just trying to read."

"Must be hard with all that noise. What are you reading?"

He lifted the book up to show me the cover: *There's Just Something About Buddhism*. "It's teaching me to be centered, and truthful and, like, stuff like that."

"Oh." I loved my brother, and he sometimes massively got on my nerves, but he was entering new territory for me here. I didn't know whether to admire him for seeking a higher truth or worry that he was sliding off into the deep end.

I turned to leave his room, and Henry said, "I wouldn't go in there if I were you." I knew he was talking about the kitchen, and Mom and Dad. "Bad energy will exhaust you."

I quietly shut his door.

In the kitchen, the argument was still going on. I was hungry, though, and wasn't about to let their issues get in the way of my need for sustenance.

"I just don't understand why you have to buy expensive cheese and *beer* when we're trying to cut back." Mom said the word "beer" as if it were a curse word.

"I wish you'd quit treating me like I don't know what I'm doing," Dad said.

"Kind of like you knew what you were doing when you did nothing to save your job?"

"How can I compete with some twenty-five-year-old kid with an MBA? It's not like I—" Dad stopped when he saw me and ran his hand through his hair. When Mom saw me, she let out a deep sigh.

"Honestly, William," Mom said, lowering her voice and trying to sound calm. "I'm just saying we have to cut back. On everything." She shook her head.

Dad looked angry but beaten. "Fine," he said through gritted teeth.

"Fine," Mom responded. "Could you please mow the lawn like you said you would while I start dinner?"

Dad shook his head and muttered, "Good Lord." He walked out the kitchen door that led to the garage, stopping to ruffle my hair on the way out.

Mom took another deep breath, then turned her attention to me. "So. What do you want for dinner? Pasta sound okay?"

I guess I was lucky that the one thing Mom knew how to make was exactly what I was in the mood for.

As the sound of the lawn mower revved up outside, Mom looked at me expectantly and said, "Well? The elections?"

I smiled. "Duh. I won."

"Congratulations! I knew you would, Lucia. And Melanie and Cooper?"

"Both in."

"Good job. Are they excited about working with you?"

"I don't know," I said.

Mom shook salt into the pot of water and said, "What does that mean?"

"I don't know. It's just—well, Melanie didn't seem excited about it. I just hope that she's into it, and takes it seriously."

"What did she say when you congratulated her on winning vice president?"

I scratched at some melted cheese on the countertop. Dad had probably made quesadillas for lunch. "Nothing."

"She didn't say anything?"

"No, *I* didn't say anything."

"Aha," Mom concluded.

"But if it weren't for me, she'd never have won the vice presidency," I argued.

"Did Melanie ask to be vice president?"

"No."

"Well, then."

I knew Mom was right. Maybe I should have been the one to congratulate her first. I should have even *thanked* her. Why hadn't I? Probably because I was too wrapped up in myself.

When Mom asked for more details about the election, I told her—about my slightly frazzled speech and how Melanie had tossed out toys to the student body. "To make matters worse," I told her, "Ms. Jenkins told me that this year's election was the closest in all her years at Angus."

"Hmm," Mom said as she poured squiggly pasta into the boiling water.

I thought about what that meant—what it really meant. "I guess part of me is relieved that I won, and maybe a little shaken that I almost lost. If Melanie had won ... well, I'd probably be pretty mad at her for beating me. But the other part of me ..."

"Yes?" Mom asked as she slowly stirred the pasta.

"I feel like nobody cares about the student council at our school but me. And it's like everybody hates me because of that. They're either barely talking to me or laughing at me about something I've done." I thought of Robbie Cordova, throwing the pirate topper at my head that morning. "But then, they go ahead and elect me for president. Even if I won by a narrow margin, I still won. It makes me think, *Well,* do *they like me?*"

Mom nodded like she understood. She'd always been a good listener. It wasn't that I was closer to her than I was to Dad; Dad had taught me all about boxing and what it took to be a champion. He always told me it took heart, but my whole heart was in politics. And even though I won, I hadn't been able to bring my passion for it to everyone else. But since Dad lost his job, I felt like he'd lost heart too. Mom nagged him for weeks before his company merged, telling him he better step up—that he should dress better, get to the office early, stay late, volunteer for extra projects. "There's another guy just like you one county away ready to take over the whole department," she'd tell him. But Dad never did any of those things, and never even bothered to worry himself about it. My dad and I used to be so tight, but not anymore. Even though he was always home, he didn't seem as available as he used to be.

"They voted for you," Mom said, "because, deep down, they trust you. And, to be honest, I think people fear change. They don't like what they don't know. Maybe they saw Melanie as someone fun, maybe a nice change of scenery, but in the end, your classmates did what people always do—they stuck with what was familiar. Now it's your job to show them that you can also shake it up, like maybe they thought Melanie did. Can you do that?"

Could I? It was only what I'd been planning since the end of the last school year. I decided I could be like Pretty Boy Floyd—I was prepared to see my presidency through to the victorious end. What else had I been training, *working* for since sixth grade?

BLUE JAYS . . .
THE VIEW FROM ABOVE

Predictable Elections Spiced Up

BY NICOLE JEFFRIES

What looked to be just another tepid student council election turned into a festive, if somewhat raucous, proceeding when presidential hopeful Melanie O'Hare showered the student body with freebies as if it were a Mardi Gras parade in New Orleans.

"I just wanted to do something a little different," Ms. O'Hare said after the assembly, her cheeks still flush with excitement. "Every year it's the same old boring speeches that nobody listens to. Some people may not agree with what I did, but hey—it sure got their attention."

When asked if she thought she had a chance of winning this year's election, Ms. O'Hare adjusted her adorable red beret and said, "To be honest, no, I don't. Lucia Latham will definitely win, and she deserves to win. I would be honored to be her vice president."

When Ms. Latham was asked the same question, she responded with, "Naturally. There's no one better qualified than I am."

Although a bit of humility might serve her well, we can't gloss over Ms. Latham's achievement. She is, after all, Angus Junior High's only three-peat president, something we hope all future Blue Jays will appreciate.

7

I won, and that was what mattered. I hadn't done anything shady to clinch my final presidency, and given my competition, I did deserve to win. Nicole's stories could be a little cutthroat, and I imagined the *Washington Post* would be glad to have her on its staff in ten years. Even though I totally didn't agree with some of the things she wrote, I did appreciate the fact that she recognized my accomplishment.

And how great was Melanie's quote? After I read that I realized that I never had to doubt Melanie. The girl was loyal.

A week after the election, I had an early-morning appointment with our principal, Ms. Jenkins, in which I planned to present to her my first—and biggest—goal of my final year at Angus. I knew it was going to be one of those things that the students didn't go crazy over right away but would (hopefully) learn to love. That's why I was doing this project first. Also, if I could get Ms. Jenkins to approve it, I would be a true trailblazer for the entire school district. No other student council president had attempted such a feat.

Of course, I was also dying to know what the big student council fund-raiser for the year would be. Each year the student councils are in charge of raising money for whatever it is the school needs, but the eighth-grade class—the top class—gets the job with the biggest dollar amount and the most responsibility. I'd mentioned to Melanie that whatever we raised money for, I was going to do a bake sale.

She wrinkled her nose and said, "Really?"

I bristled. "Yes."

"I just thought you'd want to do something a little more . . . *wow*."

"There's a reason why there've been bake sales for ages, Melanie. They're *classic*."

I needed to get to school early the next day, so I asked Cooper if I could come down to his house—which is just five houses away—to box at six instead of six thirty. He wasn't excited about getting up so early, but he agreed.

I ran in the dark across the dew-covered grass, crickets still chirping and streetlights still on. Our neighborhood was an older one, like maybe thirty years old. We all lived in tract houses—cookie-cutter homes, as my mom once said—but since they're kind of old, most people have added a porch here, a second story there, and they don't look exactly alike anymore. The Nixons have added a lot to their house since their Mexican restaurant took off, like a cool brick walk to the front door, a bay window on the side, and full-on landscaping. Melanie's house had fancy white shutters and the front door had been moved from the middle of the house to the side. Ours, though, looked like it probably had when it was first built—square, boxy, and in need of a paint job.

I got to Cooper's house just as he was opening the garage door. He yawned loudly and rubbed his eyes.

"This is cruel and unusual," he said.

"You agreed to it," I said. "Besides, it's good for you. If everyone did all the exercise we did, there wouldn't be a single diabetic person in our school. Type 2, anyway." I made a mental note to say something along those lines to Ms. Jenkins.

"I'm still sore from the other day when you went all Tyson on me." He awkwardly tried to put on his hand wraps. They were kind of hard to manage, but Dad had taught me how to wrap them right after he taught me how to jab. Cooper still hadn't learned.

"Here, give them to me," I said. As I wrapped his hands in the blue fabric (mine were black, contrasting nicely with my pink gloves), I noticed how rough his hands were, but he kept perfectly still as I worked the fabric over them. He always watched closely and I wondered, on this morning especially, why my heart pounded a little harder than usual at the feel of his breath on me. I concentrated on the wrapping, and when I was done, his hands looked like a pro's.

He punched a fist into his palm. "I think this is my favorite part," he said. "These things make me feel tough."

"You *are* tough," I said.

We put on our headgear, then tugged on our gloves and strapped the Velcro tight with our teeth. I pounded my fists together and said, "Ready for your next beating?"

Cooper cricked his neck and said, "Girl, I got moves you ain't even seen yet."

I punched the timer on the clock, leveled my gloves to my face, and said, "Let's go, then."

★

Later that morning, dressed in a knee-length khaki skirt with a pink shirt and matching Keds, I sat outside Ms. Jenkins's office, jiggling my legs, my folder balanced on my knees. I tried to hold still, remembering something Henry had said about containing your energy for positive use. Ms. Jenkins's door was shut, and the school secretary, Mrs. Weeks, who had come in just behind me, told me to wait outside her office until she was ready for me. I wondered if she was even in yet.

"We have an appointment," I told her. "Seven thirty."

"I know, Lucia," Mrs. Weeks said. "She'll be with you when she's ready."

Ms. Jenkins finally arrived ten minutes later, clutching her briefcase, folders, keys, and a cup of coffee. I couldn't help but think that if she hadn't stopped for that coffee, she'd have been here on time.

"Come on in, Lucia," she said, unlocking her office door and flipping on the lights. I grabbed the handle of my rolling backpack and followed her in. She dumped her folders and keys on her cluttered desk, turned on her computer, and sat back in her chair. "What can I do for you?"

I handed her a folder of information. "Ms. Jenkins, do you know what I did this morning?" She took a sip of her coffee and logged in to her computer. "I boxed. Just like I do at least three mornings a week. With Cooper Nixon, my new secretary. And do you know why, Ms. Jenkins?"

"Isn't your dad a boxer?"

I sat up a little straighter. "Yes. He was." I had no idea how she knew this, or why it threw me off momentarily. A flash of Dad teaching me to bob and weave raced through my mind.

"So?" Ms. Jenkins prodded.

"Oh," I said, refocusing myself. "Because of the epidemic of obesity in this country." I handed her a sheet of paper. "These are the statistics on childhood obesity. Are you aware that fifteen percent of children and adolescents in the U.S. are overweight? That's"—I referred down to my own packet—"eleven million kids. You should be horrified at that figure, because I know I am."

"Point, Lucia," she said. Ms. Jenkins often got quick and snippy with me like that, especially before she had her coffee. We'd worked together for two years, and I was used to it.

"There's something we can do, for our students now

and for future Blue Jays. I know that your hands are tied when it comes to making PE mandatory for every student, but we can tackle this obesity issue with the foods we provide our students." I passed her another stack of papers. "These are the figures for the vending machines we have as well as the nutritional value of each item, including trans fats. This here shows the nutritional values and *lack* of trans fats for the vending machines we should have." I took a quick breath, happy to see that Ms. Jenkins was looking through the material. "Okay, now I also understand that the cost of our current vending machines is pretty low. But just think—Angus Junior High could be the pilot for these machines across the entire school district. We could be the leaders of this movement." She looked interested in that, so I pressed on. I told her about the long-term risks of obesity, like high blood pressure and poor self-image. "Which is why, in the long run, it's best to invest now." Realizing that was a nice little sound bite, I decided to repeat it. "It's best to invest. Now."

I sat back and waited for her reaction. I knew she would have a ton of questions about logistics and comparison prices, but instead she dropped the handouts on her desk and sighed.

"The truth is, Lucia," she began, "I've been wanting to do something like this for some time. I just haven't had the time to come up with a solution." She smiled. "Or maybe I just haven't been creative enough."

My heart raced the fluttering beat of success.

"Okay." Ms. Jenkins clapped her hands. "I'll look at these and make sure they're the best ones for our school, especially with pricing. Did your council vote on this?"

My heart caught in my throat. "We're going to," I quickly said.

"I'd like to get this on the agenda for the next school board meeting, at the end of this week. Let me know once you've got your votes—you need three-fourths approval, correct?" I nodded.

Before I left her office, Ms. Jenkins said, "Lucia? Nice job on this one."

Here's the thing: I knew the bylaws of the student council better than anyone. I was even on the special committee in sixth grade that helped write some of the amendments. So I knew that what I'd promised was almost impossible because of two things:

Article IV, Section 4:
The student council shall meet only

```
during regularly scheduled
meetings as outlined by the advisor
at the beginning of each semester.
Unscheduled meetings may be called
only in an emergency-type situation,
with reasonable discretion.
```

What that meant, but what wasn't explicitly written, was that emergency meetings would be called only in a disastrous situation, like post tornado or school shooting. Like, a for-real emergency. And vending machines were not considered an emergency, I'm pretty sure.

The second thing I knew about the bylaws was:

```
Article VI, Section 2:
Any council vote in which money is
involved must have a one-week (seven
days) research period between presen-
tation of item and vote. Approval is
at the discretion of the principal.
```

And it was clear Ms. Jenkins didn't know this. But I didn't say anything because, honestly, at the time I was too excited about my presentation going so well. I'd spent all summer researching those machines, and in one five-minute meeting I got Ms. Jenkins's approval. That felt amazing. I guess I just thought I'd figure out the other stuff later.

The excitement of my mission accomplished faded quickly as I walked down the halls, my dilemma sitting like a brick in my stomach. I couldn't get the vote if I took the rules literally. There wasn't another school board meeting until next semester, and by then it'd be too late. The machines were supposed to be my big finish to an amazing three years as council president. If no one knew about the rules and I didn't tell anyone, was that cheating? Considering no one cared about student council, I told myself not to worry about it.

The second I got home I raced to my computer and set up our first student council meeting for the very next day.

Welcome, Team, to the eighth-grade Angus Junior High Student Council!

We have a lot of amazing tasks to tackle this year, so I hope you're ready to buckle down and work!

We'll have our first meeting TOMORROW immediately after school in our fearless leader's classroom, Mrs. Peoria's, room 245.

I have a great surprise for everyone, so make sure you arrive on time.

Humbly yours,

Lucia

The more I thought about the rules of the meeting and voting, the more incensed I became. How could our own principal not know the bylaws? I barely paused to think if Mrs. Peoria, our student council adviser in name only, knew about them. It was clear she had no interest in us at all. I realized how weary I'd become of trying to shake everyone into seeing how important and useful the student council was. When they saw those gleaming new vending machines, they'd know that Lucia Latham got stuff done.

As a test, I decided that if anyone at the meeting mentioned the bylaws, I would halt the vote and scratch the vending machine idea. Everyone had been given a copy of the rules and bylaws immediately after the election results were announced, so they were presumably informed—if they wanted to be.

After school the next day, I dashed out of last-period science and raced for Mrs. Peoria's classroom to make sure I was the first one there. I swear, Mrs. Peoria does the minimum required at this school, including the way she presents herself. Her graying hair was barely brushed, and her blouse was only kind of tucked into her slacks. I know it was the end of the day, but still. As soon as I arrived in her room, she collected some papers and a book and said she'd be in the teachers' lounge if I needed anything. "I'll be back in thirty minutes." She sighed as she dragged her feet out the door.

The first council meeting was one of my favorite parts of each year. Sure, in the past I'd had unwilling participants who sometimes made things more difficult, or even impossible for me to accomplish (see: Steven Francis), but I loved those moments before the first meeting, when I actually had myself convinced that this was the year that people understood and cared about what I did.

I arranged four desks in a circle so we could all sit facing each other. My first year as president I had held the meeting standing at the front of the classroom but felt that, after two meetings, the students were resentful of my authority, so I started doing the round table thing. It gave the illusion of us all being on equal footing.

Cooper was the first arrive, with a little smile when he saw me. He wore his standard baggy polo shirt, and his hair—which needed to be trimmed—was all mussed up in a cute kind of way. I smiled back at him. Melanie came in next, wearing a pink newsboy hat and listening to music on her MP3 player. When she saw us, she did a little shuffle.

"Did I miss anything?" she asked, taking out her earbuds.

"We're just waiting on Jared," I told her, glancing at the clock. I had avoided admitting it so far, but I was a little nervous about Jared. Only two people had run for treasurer—Jared, who mistakenly thought that being in student council got you out of homeroom, and a girl named Amanda, who failed prealgebra and ran as a dare.

I didn't have a problem with Jared per se, but I did have an uneasy feeling that he was always making fun of me. Anytime he said anything to me, there was always a bit of a smirk on his face, like he was in on something I didn't get, and he liked it that way.

Melanie popped her earbuds back in. "Hey, we should have a dance contest!" I could hear the rattling of music from across the table. "Wanna listen?" she asked Cooper, a bit loudly. She handed him a bud; he wiped it on his shirt, then tucked it into his ear. Melanie rolled her eyes but kept grooving. "Ah, yeah," she said. Cooper smiled. "Like this," she told him, and they shifted their bodies left and right in time to the music.

"Y'all," I said. I didn't want to be a buzz kill, but (a) we should have started the meeting without Jared because (b) I was anxious about getting the vote going, (c) I hated to be kept waiting and felt it was the height of selfishness, and (d) the truth was, I was a little jealous at being left out of the dance party.

The classroom door slammed, and we all turned to watch Jared saunter in. He flipped his hair out of his eyes as he sat down. "What'd I miss?"

"We've just been waiting on you," I said. I kept a pleasant but firm tone. I didn't want to put him off at our first meeting, but I also wanted to let him know that I was the boss, and he had inconvenienced us all. But if he felt bad about being ten minutes late, he didn't show it.

"Well, I do have a life," he said, dropping his books on the floor and slumping in his seat.

Almost as a prompt to everyone, I said, "Well, Article Two, Section One says all members must be on time, and those who are tardy more than twice may be up for disciplinary action."

"Are you serious, Latham? How about next time you give us more than two seconds notice before you decide to have a meeting?"

I waited for him to say more. When he didn't, I said, "Let's just get started."

Melanie, who was wrapping the earbud cords around her music player, said, "What's this big surprise you mentioned in your e-mail?"

I took a breath. I knew they wouldn't be as excited about it as I was, but as long as they voted for it, I didn't care—they'd eventually see how great the machines were. We were poised to make our mark on the entire school district, sealing our place in Angus history. Hopefully they'd think *that* was pretty cool.

"Okay, well I worked really hard on this, and it's a big deal that I know is going to be great in the long run." I paused for dramatic effect. "We're going to change out the old vending machines for new, better ones."

No one said anything. Blank. Silence. Finally, Cooper hesitantly said, "Wow. Good job, Loosh."

"So, what?" Jared said. "Does that mean you're getting us something better? Like those ice-cream vending machines?"

"Yummy!" piped in Melanie. "The ones with the ice-cream-in-the-cone thingies? What are they called?"

"Drumsticks!" cheered Jared.

"Yes! And Push-Up pops!" said Melanie.

"The *best*," agreed Jared.

"No," I said. "It's sort of an . . . alternative vending machine," I said. "With foods that are natural. Wholesome." They looked like I had just told them we were adding an extra period to the school day. "Delicious. You'll see. And we'll be the first school in the entire district to do it. We'll be pioneers!"

Jared and Melanie looked disappointed, and I felt anxious.

"What kinds of alternative foods?" Cooper asked suspiciously.

"Like, soy cheese sticks, protein cookies, and veggie chips. But they're good! I promise, you'll like them."

Jared raised his hand. It was a sarcastic move, I knew, because he wouldn't speak until I actually said his name.

"Yes, Jared?"

"Aren't we supposed to vote on this kind of stuff? I mean, this is a democracy and all, isn't it?"

"Yes, of course," I replied. "That's why I called the meeting. To present the idea and vote." I pulled three folders out of my bag, identical to the one I had given Ms. Jenkins the morning before.

"What are we supposed to do with all this?" Jared asked as I handed out the packets.

"Read it," I said. "I want everyone to be fully informed of the machines before you vote. Go through the information, and please vote via e-mail by tonight at midnight. Make sure you include everyone in the e-mail," I added, since the votes are not private.

"You expect us to read all this by tonight?" Jared moaned. "Come on, Latham. You must know we have lives." He smirked. "Some of us, anyway."

Before I could tell Jared that being condescending didn't constitute having a life, Cooper said, "I think it sounds great. Those salty corn chips and candy bars I usually eat with lunch make me feel like puking."

"Whatever," Jared said. He rolled his eyes back to me. "I just think you should give us a little more time, that's all."

Boxing teaches you that you always have to be prepared—the moment you're caught off guard, down you go. I made sure to always be prepared for anything, even for someone to call my bluff and tell me we couldn't get this done in this time frame. No one did. I said, "I understand, and I apologize for the quick turnaround time. I know everyone is busy, but once our vote goes through, Ms. Jenkins would like to put it on the school-board vote. That's why we have to do it quickly."

"We can do it," Cooper assured me, and I was so glad he spoke up. Jared still looked put out, and Melanie looked a little bored, but I was hopeful that they'd pull through as well.

I asked Cooper to please type up the meeting minutes and e-mail them out to everyone. "Tonight?" he asked.

"Well, just so everyone can be totally informed." I really didn't want to overlook anything else, since I was already on shaky ground.

After the meeting, Jared bolted out of the classroom as Mrs. Peoria wandered back in, and Melanie's sister picked her up for another trip to the mall.

"I think it's a good idea," Cooper said as we walked outside.

I looked at this guy who I'd known as long as I had memory. "Thanks for always supporting me, Coop," I said. "You always make things easier for me." I immediately felt embarrassed—we never spoke to each other about our friendship.

But it didn't seem to faze him. "You're my best friend," he said simply. "That's what best friends do, I guess."

The vote went through, just like I anticipated. Three for the new machines, one for keeping the old ones. I won't even insult your intelligence by saying who *didn't* vote for the new ones.

As soon as the final vote came in—Jared's, of course, at 11:59 p.m.—I sent an e-mail to Ms. Jenkins and told her to go ahead with putting the proposal on the school-board agenda. She wrote back that she was impressed that I got the vote done so quickly. I noted that we were both up late, working.

About a week later, Ms. Jenkins came back to me with the great news that the board had voted to try out the new machines. "We'll be the pilot school for them, and if they go over well here, they'll consider expanding them to other schools." I couldn't believe that my idea—especially one this far-reaching and big—was really going to be implemented. This was the biggest thing I'd done yet, in all my years as president. I breathed a little easier with the realization that the vote wasn't that big of a deal after all, and everything was turning out fine.

Instead, I focused on revealing the machines to the school. Ms. Jenkins took care of all the logistics of ordering them, and I was in charge of presenting them to the school. Although all the machines would be delivered at once, Ms. Jenkins agreed to only stock the one by the cafeteria until after I revealed it to the school. The others would be stocked later that day. I knew I needed to get my council involved to help them feel the enormity of this great project. So, I planned a press conference and gave everyone a job. I asked Jared to contact Nicole Jeffries to cover the unveiling for the school paper. I asked Melanie to talk to Lori Anne about taking photos. Finally, I asked Cooper to get in touch with the IT club to have them put up an announcement on the school's website. I even told him I'd write it up if he could just get it to the proper person, but he said he'd take care of it.

In my e-mail, I told everyone how important it was for us all to be there at the unveiling together, to show our solidarity and instill confidence in the students that our council was reliable. I gently reminded them that council members were required to attend two-thirds of all student council–sponsored events, which this counted as. After sending the e-mail, which I did several days before the press conference (no more last-minute stuff for me), Melanie responded, saying she'd bring a ribbon for the machine. "We can tie the ribbon around it and you and Mrs. Peoria can cut it." Which I thought was a brilliant idea—it showed creativity and initiative on Melanie's part.

I'd never felt so happy and confident about a student council year as I did then. Despite an initial hiccup in the plans, everything was working out perfectly.

Last year, at my request, the IT club set up an online poll on our school's website to vote on how the people in charge were doing at their jobs. I thought it would be a great show of checks and balances after the administration said the cheerleaders could no longer wear their uniforms on game day, causing a momentary uproar between the jocks (including coaches) and the brains (like Ms. Jenkins). That first poll showed 99 percent support of the uniforms, and by the next game, the girls proudly wore them to school. The point of the whole system was that no one was above criticism, and everyone should have a voice.

Most important to me, of course, was the student council–president rating, which stays up year-round (like the principal's rating). Everyone loves clicking on polls no matter what they're about, so whether they really gave *me* much thought, I'm not entirely sure. What I do know is that my approval rating averaged 87 percent last year.

On the morning we were to unveil the new vending machines, I went online to check my approval rating. Since I had been elected only about a month ago and hadn't yet implemented any changes, my rating was still at 100 percent. As I walked to the corner to wait for the bus, I noted, with a sense of foreboding, that I had nowhere to go but down.

Just as Cooper had promised, a blurb about our secret first project was on the school's site. I cringed, however, when I saw a typo in the copy (". . . see what this council has in stor*m* for us"). I wondered if it was Cooper's mistake or the Web people's. Either way, I hoped no one would notice.

As I waited for Melanie on the corner of our streets, shivering beneath my too-thin jacket, I tried to keep a positive spirit, hoping that she would remember to do all the things she was in charge of—bringing the ribbon for the cutting ceremony and, most important, making sure Lori Anne was there to take photographs. The night before, I'd had to use all my willpower not to call, text, or IM to remind her . . . just in case she forgot, like she did the speech. I woke up startled in the middle of the night and packed a pair of regular scissors, and because I couldn't think of anything else, I folded several rolls of wrapping paper and stuffed them into my backpack. Just in case. When I climbed back into bed, clutching Paddy, I mouthed the words to my speech until I fell asleep and dreamed about it.

Melanie came springing out her front door like always—today wearing a beat-up straw cowboy hat—and I resisted the urge to ask her if she had contacted Lori Anne and brought the ribbon. Instead, I waited for it all to unfold naturally and according to plan, like I knew it would. As the bus bounced down Great Springs Road, I listened to Melanie talk rapid-fire about the dance show she'd watched the night before.

"And that guy Koi is the *best*. You should see his moves, like, from graceful to *bam* in one beat flat. I am so totally signing up for dance," she said, her eyes gleaming with that familiar brightness they always had when she talked about something new. As she contemplated aloud the benefits of jazz, tap, ballet, and funk, I wondered if she'd try to stick it out with dance. She'd probably be pretty good at it. Really, though, I was mostly worried about the press conference and whether or not Melanie came through for me. I clutched the handle of my backpack, not even wanting to admit to myself that I had done the right thing by bringing backup paper and scissors.

"Oh, hey, is this okay?" Melanie asked, breaking into my thoughts. From her bag she pulled a folded purple sheet. She unfolded it so I could see the pattern. "I couldn't find any ribbon, but I thought this would be just as good. You can drape it over the whole machine and then yank it off like a magician when you're ready to show it to everyone. What do you think?"

My heart didn't know whether to sink or leap. Pulling a sheet off the vending machine was a great idea—it could give some flair and excitement to the event. But not *this* sheet.

"That's great," I said, taking it from her. "But Hannah Montana?"

She looked deflated. "I know. It's Beverly's. She thought it'd be funny to have them on her bed, like, to be all ironic. But then her new boyfriend came over and made fun of her for it, so it's been crumpled in her closet ever since."

I refolded the sheet, trying not to think of how the students would laugh when they saw this thing. When I tucked the sheet into my backpack, I told myself I was being a jerk. It *was* a good idea.

"Maybe I could even take hip-hop lessons," Melanie continued, tossing a few curls over her shoulder. "Or do you think that'd make me too much of a poseur? I'm not saying I want to learn to spin on my head or anything. Hey, did I ever tell you my mom used to dance?"

Startled at the mention of her mom, whom she rarely spoke about, I managed to say, "No, you didn't."

"Like, contemporary dance. In college. She always wanted to go to New York." Melanie looked straight ahead, at the road, through the driver's front window.

"That's cool," I said as we got off the bus at school. "You should really do dance. Any kind. I bet you'd be good at it."

I realized that the Hannah Montana sheet wasn't that big of a deal. Plus, I knew what Henry would say about being all obsessed with myself while Melanie talked about her mom—probably something about being reincarnated as an earthworm.

After we got our books out of our lockers, I said, "So, I'll see you in front of the caf before lunch?"

"See ya," she said.

My moments of happiness were temporarily dampened after homeroom when I bumped into Nicole.

"Hey, Nicole," I said. She stood at her locker, scratching her calf with the toe of her Teva. "You'll be there before lunch, right?"

She stopped scratching and looked at me all squinty eyed. "Do we have an interview?"

"No, the press conference. About the new vending machines I got installed?" She responded with a blank stare. "Didn't Jared talk to you about this?"

"Obviously not," she said, pulling out her lavender notebook.

I didn't want Nicole to know that any member of my staff was incompetent, so I said, "Oh, I asked him last minute. He probably just hasn't had a chance to reach out to you yet." I told her what was happening, and she agreed to come. "See you there?"

"Yeah." She yawned.

I went to U.S. history feeling pretty good about the day and the year ahead. Already I had proved that if you just work hard, good things will come your way. And even if the student body thought the vending machines were a little lame at first, they'd warm up to them, and by the end of football season, they'd forget they ever had access to greasy chips and sugary sodas. I bet our sports teams would even perform better without being loaded down with all that salt, fat, and sugar. Maybe they'd even make state this year. I jotted this thought down, thinking I could add it to my speech.

Mr. Harrison let me out of third-period U.S. history a little early so I could get to the caf and make sure everything was ready to go. I hadn't seen the machines yet—I knew them only from the pictures in the brochures. As I approached the area just outside the cafeteria, where the brand-new green-and-white machines stood, one of the janitors pulled his hand out of his pocket and was about to deposit a gleaming quarter into my machine.

"Stop!" I hollered as I ran toward him. "You can't use that!"

When he turned to look at me, I saw that it was Mickey, our head janitor.

"What's gotten into you?" he asked.

"Sorry," I said as he put the quarter back into his pocket. "I want to be the first to use it at the opening ceremony."

"Shouldn't you do a trial run first, make sure it works?"

"No. It has to be ceremonious."

Mickey shook his head. After two years together, he was used to me. I liked him because he never gave me any trouble, not even when I asked him to help me install energy-saving fluorescent bulbs in the administrative offices.

I took the Hannah Montana sheet out of my bag and shook it out. Mickey let out a low whistle. "What?" I said, even though I knew.

He kept an eye on the purple sheet as he said, "Nothing. Nothing at all."

We hung Hannah over the new vending machine, covering as much of the front as possible. I took a step back, smoothing down the front of my jeans. The black shirt and shoes I wore matched my hair perfectly, but the red jeans gave me a sense of fun and flair—not to mention red for the strength I knew the nutritious food would give everyone.

Cooper was the first to arrive, just moments after the third-period dismissal bell rang. He was out of breath and a little pink in the cheeks, and I was so happy to see him.

"That 'storm' thing on the website wasn't my fault," he said defensively.

"Coop, it's fine."

"I thought you'd be freaking out about it."

"I'm not freaking out about anything," I lied.

He seemed to relax a bit. "I ran into Nicole," he said, tugging his backpack up on his shoulder. "She's on her way."

"Was she with Lori Anne?"

"No."

"Great," I muttered, even as I tried to stay positive. The sheet was nice in theory, but what we really needed was a photographer.

There was no time to stress, because the lunch bell rang and people were starting to arrive. I put on my best face. "Hey, y'all!" I greeted as they came through the doors. "Stick around for a few minutes. We have a big ceremony starting soon!"

Finally, a crowd formed around us once Nicole and Mrs. Peoria arrived. I scanned the crowd for Lori Anne and Melanie but didn't see them anywhere. I spotted Jared standing in the back pretending to grab Ella Castleman's butt—she was a cute cheerleader who didn't know what the EU was. I caught his eye, then motioned for him to come up and stand with me. Max Rowe, who I hadn't noticed before, apparently thought I was waving to him, because he gave me an enthusiastic wave back *and* a thumbs-up. I forced a smile before pointing to Jared. Max nudged him—a bit hard—and I again motioned for Jared to come up. With a roll of his eyes, he made his way up front.

When Mrs. Peoria arrived, she looked at her watch and said, "Okay, Lucia. Let's get this going."

I anxiously searched again for Lori Anne—I'd all but given up on Melanie. I knew I should have just asked Lori Anne to come myself. You have to be willing to make adjustments in the blink of a jab, but I still didn't like the unexpected.

Just as I told Mrs. Peoria I was ready, Lori Anne came pushing through the crowd.

"A little notice would have been nice," she muttered, pulling her camera out of its case. Looking at Cooper, she said, "Next time, I may not come."

Cooper snapped his cell phone shut and jammed it into the pocket of his baggy jeans. He must have just texted her—I wanted to hug him for it as much as I wanted to yell at Melanie.

"We're so glad you could make it," I said as she readied her camera. "We really appreciate it."

"Oh, brother," Jared muttered beside me.

"Hello, everyone! Hello!" I said in a loud but pleasant voice to get everyone to quiet down. "Thank you for joining us today on this momentous occasion. Today we are bringing something fresh and exciting to our school." I noticed Nicole scribbling in her book, and Lori Anne snapped a couple of pictures. "Everyone gets tired and sluggish throughout the day. I know I do! So my team and I thought long and hard about what we could do to help every student and teacher—every member of the Angus Junior High team, in fact"—I smiled at Mickey, who didn't notice because he was diligently picking lint off his shirt—"live up to his or her full potential, both in terms of academics and sports. Today is the first day that all Angus Blue Jays can start performing like the champions I know we all are. So!" I took hold of the edge of the purple sheet. "Without further ado, I give you, Naturally Natural Foods!" I ripped Hannah Montana from the machine with a flourish, as Lori Anne continued to snap pictures. With my arms outstretched in a *ta-da!* pose, I waited for the applause that I thought would logically follow such a speech. Finally, Cooper started clapping, and others (begrudgingly) followed suit.

I dropped the sheet to the side, and Cooper quickly scooped it up and rolled it into a bundle in his arms. "And now, if I may, Mrs. Peoria"—I looked to our student council adviser, who was staring glassy-eyed out the side window—"I'd like to be the first to try one of these delicious snacks."

I pulled the change I had precounted from the front pocket of my red jeans and dropped it into the slot. I made a big show about deciding which snack to choose—carrot and celery chips? organic chocolate-coconut spelt bar? flax-seed crackers with amino acids and omega-3?—then finally settled on the one I wanted all along, the organic wheat- and dairy-free fig bar. There was a moment of panic as I waited for the granola bar to thump down into the slot; when it did, I let out a little breath of relief and saw that Cooper did too. Our eyes caught, and we smiled at each other.

I held up the granola bar so Lori Anne could get a shot of me, then I unwrapped it. "Let's see how it tastes!" I bit into the bar and slowly chewed. "Mmm ... delicious *and* nutritious!" I kept chewing, and Lori Anne kept snapping shots. "Well," I said through slow bites, "thanks for coming, and enjoy your lunch. And snacks!"

The crowd dispersed and headed into the cafeteria. A couple of curious people went to examine the machine, but no one purchased anything. It was, after all, right before lunch.

"Great job," Cooper said. "I think Lori Anne got a lot of good shots." He looked at me funny and said, "You okay?"

I finally couldn't take it anymore. With no napkin and no trash can around, I ducked to the side of Naturally Natural Foods and spit what was left of the dry granola bar into the wrapper in my hand, stifling down coughs and gags. Bits of oat were embedded in my molars, and I dug my fingernail into them, the dry texture combined with the mushy fig threatening to make me puke. "Oh my God," I said to Cooper, but making sure no one else was around. "That is the worst thing I have ever tasted in my life."

Cooper looked at me with wide eyes. "Seriously?" I nodded. "You think that means we're in for it?"

I forced what was left in my mouth down my throat. My eyes were watery from coughing and trying to swallow what basically amounted to shredded cardboard.

Cooper looked at me with a mix of concern and fear in his eyes.

"No," I answered defiantly. "Never."

BLUE JAYS . . .
THE VIEW FROM ABOVE

Rage Against the Vending Machine

REPORTED BY NICOLE JEFFRIES

Student council president Lucia Latham carried out her first order of business as president by presenting a new—and supposedly improved—vending machine to the halls of Angus.

The first of three machines was revealed on Tuesday to much fanfare and hype. The machine stayed covered in a purple Hannah Montana cloth sheet, obviously meant to symbolize the pure yet supposedly fun and popular food she was about to reveal. Ms. Latham extolled its virtues—among them, the promise for more energy and success in both academics and athletics.

"These products behind me," she

boasted, "will help every student at Angus live up to his or her potential." When it was finally time for the reveal, many expected something more exciting than health food.

"I thought it was going to be the new Total Destruction energy drinks and carb bars," said seventh grader Andre Franco, who runs track and cross-country. "At least maybe some of those gel packs."

"I was disappointed," admitted eighth grader Samantha Thibodeaux. "With the way her speech was going, I thought she was going to reveal some super-powered computer or something. Health food was the last thing I expected. Or wanted," she added gravely.

By press time, only a handful of students had sampled the health-food fare. Sixth grader Gina Cameron, who sampled the carob-iced spelt doughnut, called it "barely edible," while eighth grader Robbie Cordova was more blunt:

"It made me want to hurl," he said of the whole wheat carob cake. "I wouldn't feed it to my obese cat, and she has a compulsive eating disorder."

At press time, Ms. Latham had not responded to phone calls and e-mails questioning the quality of the foods. Now, only time will tell if the machines are a costly mistake—a costly one for Ms. Latham, and the pockets of our school.

10

"Um, pardon me, but hasn't she ever heard of unbiased reporting? This is the second article Nicole has put out that's totally roasted me."

Melanie and I were sitting on the trampoline at Cooper's house, a copy of the *View from Above* between us.

"It's not as bad as you think," said Melanie as she folded up the school paper and looked at a story on the back page about cell phones in class.

"I just can't believe she didn't even give me a chance to respond. Forgive me for going to the store with my mom!" I said. "I asked Mrs. Troxel if I could respond in my own words on the school's website, but she went into some bull about how I couldn't suddenly become a journalist and write about myself. Like she's never heard of Op-Ed?"

I took back the paper and looked at the story again. The above-the-fold picture showed Cooper, Jared, and me standing smiling beside the big green machine. The caption had our names from left to right, and then read, *Not pictured, Vice President Melanie O'Hare*. It was a slap in the face, both from Melanie and Nicole. Like she really had to write that.

"Hey," I said, nudging Melanie's foot. "What happened that day, anyway?" She pulled a stray hair off her shoulder, held it between her fingers, then released it into the wind. "Why weren't you there with us?"

"Oh my gosh, I never told you!" she burst. "I almost lost my vision that day."

"What?"

"I swore that, like, a piece of glass was in my eye, scratching it to death. I had to go to the nurse and everything." She leaned back on her hands and looked off toward the street. Story finished.

"Well, what was it? Are you okay?"

"Yeah, the nurse gave me some saline to wash my eye out with, and then it was fine. But by then this whole thing was over." She gestured to the paper.

"Oh. Well, I'm glad you're okay." That's what I said, but inside I was fuming. What a lame excuse. She really had no idea how important the vending machines were to me, or what it took to get them installed. Or that everyone else took the time to be there as a united council, even if *some* people (Jared!) did it grudgingly.

"Well, the good news," Melanie said, "is now that this thing is over, you can start concentrating on the big fund-raiser bake sale deal. You know what you're raising money for yet?"

"They haven't said." The fact that she said "you're," not "we're," did not escape me.

Over Melanie's shoulder I saw Cooper carrying out snacks to us: a wooden bowl of fresh guacamole and his dad's homemade tortilla chips, two Dr Peppers, and a bottle of water.

"Just relax, Lucia," Melanie said. "Look at the big picture. Don't read too much into this."

"Humph," I said as Cooper hopped up, making us bounce gently like we were in a boat on water. I had a hard time listening to her halfheartedly cheer me up about something she'd ditched me on. So I looked at Cooper and said, "What about the article she ran after the election? She said I needed a little *humility.*" When they didn't answer, I sighed and ate a chip.

Yes, I knew it was ironic to be eating fried chips while reading about my health-food vending machines, but all things in moderation, right? Besides, Cooper's dad made the best tortilla chips. They were impossibly yummy, with the perfect amount of salt and a *zing* of lime.

"Did you make this?" I asked, scooping fresh guacamole onto a chip. Cooper nodded.

Cooper settled himself in, and I placed the bowl back on the trampoline. Even though we all lived within a few houses of each other, the three of us rarely hung out together. Mel and Cooper were friends because I was friends with each of them. Mel was usually either shopping or out with one of her other friends, and Coop was either with Max or at the restaurant. When we were all together, they were cordial but never more than that.

"She's right," Cooper said, popping open his drink. "It's not that big a deal. And Nicole doesn't say anything really bad here."

"It's not what she says, but implies," I said. A flash of my own deceit in getting these machines placed zipped across my mind; I quickly told myself it was old news. "This article is planting the seed into the students' minds that they shouldn't trust me." Without meaning to, I shot a look at Melanie. She busied herself with picking out the tiniest crumbs of chips and eating them one by one.

"Have you looked at the online polls yet?" Cooper asked. "See if they posted anything about this?"

"Oh, I love those surveys," Melanie said, bouncing. I grabbed my drink just before it spilled. "I like the fun ones that ask, like, Which is the best last song to play at a dance?"

"Yeah," Cooper said. "The choices were, like, Backstreet Boys, that disco song, or a sing-along."

"I voted for the Backstreet Boys," Melanie said.

"Gross! Those old guys? My *mom* likes them."

"I was being ironic," she said.

"Right."

I loaded up another chip with guacamole. I could only imagine what the poll questions about me would be. *Is Lucia Latham the worst president ever?*

As Melanie and Cooper debated cheesiest last songs, I said, perhaps a bit forcibly, "So, y'all are saying I'm totally overreacting?" Melanie made a playful swat at Cooper when he asked her if she thought Barry Manilow was hot. I sighed and said, "I guess so."

Melanie perked up and said, "Hey, I know. Why don't you get a crazy new haircut?" When she didn't say more, I raised my eyebrows and waited. "You know. Bleach that dark hair white blond. To divert attention. The public is always interested in how the girl politicians look, so if you get some weird new 'do, then they'll probably have a Love It/Hate It poll on your hair instead of what you're doing."

"Humph." She just might be right on that. I tried to imagine my dark hair bleached out like so many celebrity girls'. But I'd never stoop to those levels. As far as I was concerned, gender had no role in politics.

Melanie turned back to Cooper. "Sometimes at night, I just lie awake thinking of all the new polls the school site should do. Like, they should do those 'Marry, Kiss, or Kick' surveys for the teachers—you have to pick which one you'd marry, one you want to kiss, and the last one you get to smack." She gave a shameful version of a jab. "Pow!"

Cooper laughed. "Awesome! Who would be on it?"

Melanie thought for a moment. "Okay, your choices are: Mrs. Peoria, Ms. Jenkins, and Coach Ryan."

"Ugh! A cat worshipper, an uptight old lady, and a dude? Come on!" Cooper said.

As I watched them debate, I thought about how I didn't want people to think I'd messed up. I had to be a success. I'd gone so far as to push the vote through to make sure I was. It wasn't enough to be the school's first three-peat president, or to spearhead the district's first alternative vending machine. If I got lazy and did nothing more, then everyone's totally false opinion of the council—that we did nothing—would be true. I couldn't get lazy and let things coast; I had to keep pushing forward. It's like Dad used to say about boxing: By the third round you're already tired, like you can't throw another punch, but that's the exact time you have to really get your fight on. After all, the other guy is probably tired too. Why not take the advantage and push forward?

As Melanie and Cooper debated over who would make the best spouse ("I hear Coach Ryan makes killer barbecue," Melanie teased), I started to wonder what people wanted from me. More stuff? Different stuff? To be left alone? Now that was a poll I'd like to have posted. I'd title it, "Just What the Heck Do You Want from Lucia Latham, Anyway?" Might make my life easier.

Cooper and Melanie finished the guacamole and started throwing chips at each other. I watched as Melanie grabbed a handful, crushed them in her palm, then tossed them like confetti over Cooper. She laughed out loud when Cooper pelted her between the eyes, and when she tried to throw a chip back, he caught her by the wrist, which made her laugh even louder, and him, too. A power struggle began, and soon they were falling practically on top of each other, spilling soda all over the trampoline. I jumped up to keep from getting any on my jeans.

"Y'all, be careful!" I said—okay, maybe nagged.

Cooper tossed the empty wooden bowls to the grass. "Just bounce it off," he said of the drinks and crumbs.

As Melanie and Cooper jumped, I stood still, which is hard to do on a trampoline. I watched them laugh, so carefree, and wondered if something was changing— either with them, or with me. Melanie's red, yellow, and green knit Rasta hat stayed perfectly placed on her head, even in flight.

Melanie took my wrist. "Come on!" she cheered, bouncing hard next to me. Cooper grabbed my other wrist and soon they were pulling me up with them, the three of us jumping in unison. I finally cracked a smile, momentarily forgetting all my problems. Watching Melanie, I realized that fun things always seemed to happen when she was around.

"Whoever thinks Lucia Latham is the best president Angus Junior High ever had," Melanie yelled to me, Cooper, and the entire neighborhood, "say aye!"

As Cooper and Melanie both yelled "Aye!" at the tops of their lungs, Melanie pulled off her Rasta hat and tossed it across the yard with such abandon that I couldn't help but feel a little jealous. The lightness in her was visible as she floated above us both, toward the sky.

11

"What are you guys doing for dinner?" I asked Melanie as we walked home later that evening. It was dark, and the streetlights were on, crickets chirping in the grass. I pulled my light jacket tight against the cold night air. I had hoped Cooper's mom would invite us to stay for dinner, but she didn't.

"Dad's been working late, so yesterday Bev and I got one of those family-sized boxes of shells and cheese. Rose is coming over and we're going to pig out and watch whatever is on Bravo. Mom would die if she knew we were eating like this." She laughed, but not in a ha-ha sort of way.

I felt a pang in my stomach. Melanie's dad rarely ate with them, mostly because he was rarely around. He worked long hours and gave Melanie and her sister a ton of freedom and little responsibility. Now that Beverly could drive (and she drove a nicer car than my parents did), one of their "chores," Mel said, was doing the weekly grocery shopping. I went with them once—Mr. O'Hare gave them his credit card, and they basically went wild, grabbing whatever they wanted. If they were unsure if they were out of popcorn or shredded cheese, they'd just get more. They mostly bought junk food and frozen dinners, but they also bought pink mascara, tons of nail polish, tabloids, picture frames, colored pens, and bags of candy. The day I went with them, I was both jealous and a little incensed at their wastefulness. Like they really needed three more bottles of nail polish, and that pink mascara cost almost ten bucks. Meanwhile, I had run out of my eucalyptus-and-ginger scrub, and although I really wanted to ask Mom to buy more, I realized I didn't *really* need it.

When I got home it was quiet, as usual, but Mom's car was in the driveway, so I figured she was in her room reading or something. I stayed in my room doing home-work, feeling more secure about the vending machines after hanging out with Cooper and Melanie. I even told myself I was glad Cooper and Mel seemed to be getting friendlier with each other. We could all walk through the doors of high school next year, shoulder to shoulder.

Then Mom called—make that yelled—for everyone to come to dinner.

Dad was already sitting at the head of the table, and Henry sat on the edge of his seat, back straight, shoulders relaxed, with his hands in what he told me was the mudra position—palms in front of him with his thumbs and forefingers joined. He said it was this special way of sitting that guarantees you'll never have a tense muscle in your body. If you ask me, teaching people how to sit is a crock.

I sat down, muttering a hello to Dad, noticing he hadn't shaved.

"Hey, girl," he said, giving me a weary smile.

"Growing a beard?" I asked just before the oven door slammed and Mom stomped over to the dining area. She practically dropped the casserole dish of lasagna on the table.

"Christ, Janey," Dad said, but Mom just went back into the kitchen and brought out a salad bowl, and plopped that down next to the lasagna.

She slapped food onto our plates, and Henry and I eyed each other. We knew better than to say a word.

"I just can't believe . . . ," she said under her breath, then shook her head.

We ate in fear. Even Henry wasn't sitting on the edge of his chair anymore—his back was hunched and his ears were practically resting on his shoulders. Thinking I could help, I said, "Wow, Mom. This is the best lasagna you've made in a while."

When she plunked down her fork, I knew I'd made a mistake. "You think? That's really sweet of you, Lucia. Because I worked really hard this evening to make it. And the ingredients weren't cheap. And I had to go into work at seven o'clock this morning so that I could leave at a decent enough hour so that we could all eat this dinner *that I have cooked* together."

"Janey—," Dad said through clenched teeth.

"Just don't," Mom said, pointing her finger at Dad like she used to do to me when I back-talked. "I don't want to hear it. I can't believe you turned down that job. It's like a bad joke."

"I'm not some minimum-wage cook, Janey," he snapped.

"That is not what John offered you and you know it. *William*," she added.

Henry and I exchanged looks again. Henry mouthed, *The Nixons?* I discreetly shrugged and mouthed, *I guess*.

Cooper's dad must have offered Dad a job at their restaurant.

"It's not what I do," Dad said, darting his eyes between Henry and me.

If anyone had asked my opinion, I would have said that I agree with Dad. If Mr. Nixon *was* offering Dad some cooking position, what made him think he was qualified? Dad was a boxer-turned-accountant, and neither had anything to do with perfecting a molé sauce. I looked at my dad's weary face, and even though I really wanted him to fix this situation, I knew that Mom rode him pretty hard for a reason. She was like his trainer, pushing him to work when he felt like quitting to get home in time to watch the football game. Dad needed to work, but he didn't want to, so Mom was trying to make him want it.

"Not what you do? Well, then," Mom said, exasperated. I hated it when they fought in front of us. I'm pretty sure there's something in Parenting 101 that says you should never fight in front of the kids. "I'll continue to do everything around here until the perfect job just lands in your—"

"Enough," Dad said. He looked at Henry and me as if

to remind Mom we were there. For that, I was grateful.

Mom sighed and dug into her dinner, spearing each bite. "Lucia, Henry," she said. "I need to cut your chore money down. At least for a while."

"Okay," I muttered, not wanting to upset Mom any more than she already was.

"We're cutting back on everything," she continued, keeping her eyes on her plate. "You're still expected to do your chores." I guess I let out a sigh or a moan or some sort of noise, because Mom snapped, "And no attitude!"

I clenched my jaw and kept my eyes on my half-eaten dinner. I sort of got that Dad didn't want to take a job that had nothing to do with his skill set, or whatever, but I couldn't help but think, *He's the adult*. He's supposed to take care of us. And he's burdening Mom every day. Didn't Dad know that he was the reason Henry had started those breathing exercises? The meditation? The sitting positions that were supposed to relieve muscle tension? A ten-year-old shouldn't be that stressed, even a kid genius who skipped second grade and was still in all honors classes.

Dad reached across the table and rested his hand on top of mine; I snatched it away. I hadn't meant to react so sharply, but there it was.

I avoided looking at him when I asked, "May I be excused?"

"Rinse your plate," Mom said.

Back in my room, I laid on my bed, clutching Paddy and staring at the wall. I wanted to understand Dad. I didn't know what it was like to have a real job and support a family, but I did know what it was like to work hard and have people depend on you.

Dad used to be a fighter; he used to train hard every day, sometimes twice a day, to be the best junior middleweight fighter he could be. I never thought about his job as an accountant, but I couldn't imagine anything being further removed from boxing than that. What if what I loved doing was taken away from me? I clutched Paddy and tried to think of a scenario in which my presidency could be snatched away from me without my permission. My bending the rules wasn't exactly a high point in my presidency, but it wasn't so bad that it would destroy me. Dad had always taught me to fight for what I wanted, and to keep fighting until I got it. But he wasn't fighting anymore. He wasn't even trying.

A poll about the vending machines appeared two days later. I was surprised it took that long—the school's server must have been down or something.

**WHAT DO YOU THINK OF THE NEW
VENDING MACHINES?**

5 – Delicious! I could eat from them every day!

4 – There are one or two things I like to buy from them.

3 – I haven't tried them yet.

2 – I tried them once and didn't like what I got.

1 – The food is horrible and I haven't met one person who likes them.

A whopping 75 percent selected answer number one. But I didn't need a poll to tell me that people hated the food. If you just walked by one you could see for yourself. Someone had wrapped the one by the cafeteria in fake biohazard tape. CAUTION! it read. TOXIC INGRE-DIENTS! On the machine by the front lobby, someone taped a printout of a skull and crossbones. Oh, sure, someone always took it down—usually me—but it was always back up the next day.

Most of the old vending machines had been returned to the company we'd leased them from, but somehow one lone old machine was in the coaches' temporary offices on the edge of the athletic fields. Word in the halls was that the candy and chips in it were now hot items. Melanie said she heard a rumor that Coach Fleck had the key to it and had become the school's black-market dealer, stocking the machine himself—and keeping the profits. She said he was running himself a fine little business out there. When I asked her if she'd ever bought anything from him, she conveniently had a coughing fit.

Before I could come up with a solid course of action, Ms. Jenkins said she wanted to meet with me.

I kept positive thoughts, telling myself it would be a good day despite the cold wind that blew prematurely fallen leaves across our front lawn. After combing my hair, I rolled my backpack through the dark living room toward the kitchen. I stopped in the middle of the living room, spotting a huge lump on the couch. As my eyes adjusted, I realized it was Dad. His bare foot hung off the end and his back was twisted at an awkward angle. I wanted to think he'd fallen asleep watching TV, but it looked pretty deliberate.

In the kitchen, I poured a bowl of generic Bran Bites (which were growing on me), and Mom came in to make the coffee.

"So," I said, trying to act like I wasn't freaked out. "What's Dad doing on the couch?"

"Oh." She paused for a quick moment as she took her IntraWorks coffee mug out of the cabinet. "I was up late reading and the light was bothering him, so he came out here to sleep."

I told myself this was totally reasonable. Mom was always reading or working, and who could sleep with a light on? Not me, probably.

At school, when Ms. Jenkins was ready to see me, I entered her office and parked my backpack against the wall, lowering the handle as I did so. When I sat down, I told myself that this was just a meeting between two colleagues to discuss options—no, *new opportunities*. She probably just wanted to brainstorm.

"Lucia," Ms. Jenkins began, her voice a little stern for a colleague-to-colleague chat, "it's not working."

She didn't even have to preface herself. My stomach churned even as I told myself that every problem has a solution.

"I don't even think anyone is using the machines," she said, digging through papers on her desk. It was like she wasn't even talking to me. "We had to restock the other machines every two weeks, but maintenance says they haven't needed to yet. We need a solution, and quick." She didn't seem to find whatever she'd been looking for on her desk, but she finally looked up at me. Was that panic I saw in her eyes?

An absurd thought flashed through my mind—I was glad Nicole wasn't around to hear this. The last thing I needed was more bad publicity in *View from Above*.

"Well," I began, telling myself I could help the situation, and Ms. Jenkins. "I haven't seen the sales stats yet. But I'm sure if we just give the machines—and the student body—some time, people will get used to them and see how great they are. They'll see how much better they feel, how much more energy they have—"

"I don't have time," she said, shaking her head. "I'm starting to think I made a huge mistake in doing this." She said "*I* made a huge mistake," but what I heard was "*You* made a huge mistake."

"Lucia, I called you in here to ask that you and your council come up with some possible solutions. The school board president is down my throat about this because it's so costly." I realized then that Ms. Jenkins might actually be freaking out. Which made me feel freaked out. "The school is losing money," she said. "Vending machines are an important source of income for us. Do you understand?"

I wasn't sure that I understood, but what my mind told me was that if we—if I—didn't come up with a solution, Ms. Jenkins would lose her job. All because of me.

Two nights later, a new poll was on the school website:

Which vending machine would you rather have in the halls of Angus?
- The healthy machines. The food takes some getting used to, but it makes me feel great!
- The old ones! With so little to look forward to

at school, those Snickers bars really help get me through the day.

The vote was 92 percent for the old machines. I wondered who the 8 percent was that voted the other way. Probably someone who had nothing better to do than skew the polls. And, okay, I admit I did vote more than once for the healthy food, but not more than five times, so it wasn't just me who made up that 8 percent. I wondered if Cooper had helped, or maybe even Melanie.

I clutched Paddy, my only source of comfort these days, willing myself to believe this.

The next day, and for a week after that, I started using what was left of my meager chore money to buy food from the vending machines. It wasn't exactly the solution Ms. Jenkins was looking for, but it was all I had at the time. I bought a carob-iced spelt doughnut first thing in the morning, and I always got carrot and celery chips on my way into the cafeteria. I'd ask to go to the bathroom in several of my classes throughout the day to buy a chocolate gilk (goat's milk) or Sogurt (soy yogurt). I put the food in a cloth bag in my locker; by the end of one week, it was filled to capacity, and a month's worth of chore money was already gone. I couldn't keep it up alone. It was financially impossible.

At home that evening, I sat on my bed and tried to come up with a game plan while eating some cheese puffs I'd found in the back of the pantry. As I wrote and ate I had to keep licking the orange flecks off my fingers. Even though they were loaded with trans fats, they were tasty, and besides, I couldn't take any more health food.

I sat on my bed with Paddy beside me and wrote and scratched out ideas. I wondered if I could hold some sort of boxing exhibition, maybe teach students the basic moves for a small fee, the money going toward the machines. No one at school except Cooper knew that part of me—I wondered what everyone would think if they knew? Would they think I was a freak? Would they think it was cool? As I pictured myself showing Lily Schmidt how to throw herself into an uppercut, and gaining more confidence as she did so, another image appeared of someone accidentally clocking sweet, quiet Lily in the jaw, sending her to the shiny wood floor of the gym, out cold.

As I worked out other ways to make people use the machines and save my approval rating, Cooper called, inviting me to come down and box.

"It's weird," he said over the phone, "but I feel great

lately. Like, lots of energy, and my mind has been so sharp, like I could work all day. And the only thing I'm doing differently is eating from those vending machines."

Cooper was the worst liar, but I played along. Just knowing he was trying to make me feel good set me at ease, at least a little.

Down at his house, I wrapped my hands, then started on Cooper's. I turned his hand flat, working the fabric around his wrist, then up across this palm. As I worked the wrap through his fingers, giving him extra protection across his knuckles—even though he would never hit me hard—I realized that I probably knew his hands better than any other girl did. Maybe even better than he knew them. He always had rough spots across his knuckles, and his right index finger crooked slightly to the left from when he broke it in fourth grade catching a basketball. And like every time I wrapped his hands, we didn't talk, but this time, up close, I noticed that he had a little splattering of freckles on his nose. They looked nice on him.

When I finished we pulled on our gloves and set the timer, and Cooper bounced more lightly on his feet than usual. He cricked his neck as if he were about to fight for the heavyweight championship of the world.

"You're going down!" he cheered as we started the round.

In the past, when I felt down about something, boxing helped get me out of the funk. I looked forward to shoving all that negative energy out of my body and getting my thoughts focused again. But that didn't happen this time. I just felt tired. Cooper swung a lot of fakes at me, waiting for me to hit. I took a few swings, and even landed a couple of soft punches to his arms, but it wasn't the same. I just went through the motions of pushing my arm forward and pulling my body away.

"Come on," he cheered, punching his glove just before my face. "Fight back!"

In the middle of the second round, I lowered my gloves. I had worked up a mild sweat, but my heart wasn't in it, and my head was somewhere else.

"Oh, fine." Cooper relented. "Want something to eat?"

Ever since Mr. Nixon had started up his restaurant, their house always smelled of delicious, spicy foods cooking and simmering and baking. Their large kitchen, which was filled with top-notch appliances, spilled into the living room, so whenever someone was cooking, you always felt a part of it. It looked nothing like our kitchen, which was its own isolated room and had a broiler that hadn't worked in months. It drove my mother crazy, but she said there were better things to be doing with our money, like trying to keep up with the mortgage.

At the Nixons' there was a counter between the kitchen and the living room, and Cooper and I parked ourselves at it on the living-room side and leaned over, watching Mr. Nixon stir something in a big, shiny pot. The scent alone made me glad I had come over.

"How's that coming?" Cooper asked his dad.

Still stirring, Mr. Nixon turned to look at us. When he saw me, a smile as big as the pot spread across his face. "Well, hello there, Lucia. How are you, honey?"

"I'm fine," I said, feeling warm and relaxed. "Whatcha making?"

"This here," he said, "is a new tortilla soup I'm trying out."

"I had some yesterday," Cooper said, "but I said it needed some honey and jalapeño in it."

"Yep," his dad agreed. "Spice and sweet. Y'all ready to test this out?"

"Sure!" Cooper and I cheered.

Mr. Nixon's name was John, and he always insisted that I call him that, but it felt funny, calling an adult by his first name, even if I had known him since I was born. I usually just ended up not calling him anything.

Mr. Nixon set down two steaming bowls in front of us. "Now hang on," he said, shuffling around in the kitchen. He turned back and placed a large soupspoon at the side of both of our bowls, then topped our soup with red, black, and yellow tortilla strips. "Dig in, and tell me what you think. Be honest! I can take it."

Cooper and I blew gently on the soup in our spoons, then delicately sipped the broth. It was wonderful. I think it was the honey that Cooper suggested that made it so outstanding—that little sweet kick made all the difference.

Cooper and I looked at each other and said, "So good!"

"Really?" Mr. Nixon asked. "You wouldn't fool an old man, would you?"

"No way, Dad," Cooper said. "This is awesome."

"Okay, then. To the menu it goes!" Mr. Nixon said, reaching into his back pocket and pulling out his wallet. I watched curiously as he handed over a ten-dollar bill to Cooper. "Good job, son."

Cooper shoved the money into his pocket, telling me, "Consulting fee. Whenever I come up with an idea he uses, I get paid. Ten for food ideas, and five for in-house ideas."

"Wow," I said, truly impressed. "Nice business skills, Coop."

"Lucia, how's your daddy doing?" Mr. Nixon asked as Cooper and I continued to dig into our soup.

I swallowed the bite I had just taken. "He's fine," I answered. I didn't know if he knew that I knew about the job offer, but I sure wasn't going to mention it, and I hoped he wouldn't either. Thankfully, just then the phone rang.

"Haven't heard from him in a few days," he said, as if waiting for me to say more.

"He's always home," I said, trying to sound casual. "Just come on down." I could feel Cooper's eyes on me, like he was waiting to see if I would explode or something.

"Cooper!" his mom called from the bedroom. "It's Melanie!"

I turned my head to him. "For you?"

He shrugged but didn't look at me. He took the kitchen phone but walked around the corner, into their dining room.

I stirred my soup, wondering why Melanie was

calling Cooper. Maybe they had the same teacher for one of their classes and she was calling about homework? As I played with my food, I thought about the other day on the trampoline and wondered if they'd actually been flirting. I shook that thought out of my head. Besides, I couldn't help but feel that Cooper was *my* friend, not Melanie's.

"School going okay for you?" Mr. Nixon asked as he poured the remaining soup into a storage bowl.

"Yes, sir," I said automatically. I tried to hear what Cooper was saying on the phone but could get only bits and pieces as he paced into and out of my view. When I caught a glimpse, he was biting his lip and muttering, "Uh-huh," a lot. What was she saying to make him smile like that? And when did he get those calf muscles?

"They say the friends you make in your teenage years tell everything about how you'll be in life," Mr. Nixon continued. "'Course, I don't think we have to worry about you."

I wanted to say, *Phew. If you only knew. Currently I'm totally messing up the biggest venture of my career with those vending machines—a prelude to my future in politics?—and meanwhile my two best friends are on the phone talking about God knows what, and I sort of want to kill someone because everything in my life seems to be completely out of order.*

Instead, I took another bite of the soup, but now I tasted neither spicy nor sweet. More like bitter.

Finally, Cooper finished his call and put the cordless back in its cradle. He sat down next to me but didn't look at me.

"What was that about?"

"Nothing," he said.

"Has she called you before?"

He shrugged. "Yeah."

"Y'all call each other?"

"Yeah, sometimes. Why? It's not a big deal, Loosh."

"I know," I said, feeling defensive, but all I could think was, *What the heck?* Trying to sound like I didn't care, I said, "I just didn't know y'all were friends, you know, outside the three of us. That's all."

"Well," Cooper said, "we are."

There was a bit of finality in that. He was telling me to back off. He'd never done that before.

"Fine. Sorry I asked."

Cooper finished the last of his soup. "Thanks, Dad," he said, setting it on the counter. "It was great."

"Yeah, thanks," I said, doing the same. Mr. Nixon took our bowls and rinsed them in the sink.

"I better get going," I said to Cooper. Melanie's call made me feel funny in a way I couldn't—or didn't want to—put my finger on. All I knew was that I needed to get out of there, go home, and be alone. I didn't even want to go back to the garage and get my gear. I just wanted out.

"Okay," Cooper said as we walked to the front door. "Hey, you want to jump on the trampoline for a while?"

"No, thanks," I said. Even when Cooper was the one making me upset, he was still the one trying to make me feel better. "I should get home and shower."

"Yeah, I guess I should too," he said at the front door. "Shower, I mean."

I started down the brick walk, past the just-planted shrubs. "Hey, Loosh?" Cooper called. I turned back to him. "Everything's cool. Right?"

I nodded, but I got the feeling that he was just saying what he thought I wanted to hear. Which meant that even he knew everything wasn't okay.

"I don't think my life could get any worse," I told Melanie on the bus ride to school. I opened a Pop Tart imposter and bit through the dry pastry. Not only had all brand names disappeared from our kitchen, but a lot of my healthy food had too. But that was the least of my problems. This whole thing with Melanie calling Cooper the night before had totally thrown me. Why did I care so much? Did I want him to grab my wrist the way he had grabbed hers that day on the trampoline? I wasn't sure, but I thought if I confided in Melanie, she might confide in me.

"Come on, Lucia. Things aren't that bad."

I looked out the window as we left the neighborhood and entered the main road to school. When I got home from Cooper's the night before, I'd even tried to kiss my elbow to see if I'd turn into a boy. Sad, right?

"I know. But I mean, well—you've seen what they've done to the vending machines. Have you bought anything from them yet?"

Melanie wore a green knit beanie with a little ball on top, and I wondered if there was anything she didn't look totally adorable in. "I haven't, but I swear I will," she said. "I never have any money on me."

I held my tongue. Maybe if the machines took credit cards, she would have bought a ton by now. "So, what's new with you? Anything exciting happening?" It sounded like obvious digging, but Melanie didn't seem to notice.

She shrugged. "I'm thinking about taking dance."

"Still just thinking?"

"Well, not regular dance. More like Irish dancing. You know—like in those touring dance shows? Irish jig, that sort of thing."

I shouldn't have been surprised, but I always was. "Why?"

She pointed to her hat, like that solved everything. Then she said, "My mom was Irish."

I wanted to ask more, maybe just ask her directly if she had a crush on anyone, but I was too afraid of learning the truth. I knew I could never be a reporter. Nicole would have had an answer from her by the time the bus rounded the first corner.

When we got to school, Melanie asked, "We still having a student council meeting after school?"

"Yep," I said. "Mrs. Peoria's room right after last bell."

I watched Melanie walk away, her thick curly hair resting against her back, the beanie lying against it. She glanced back and said, "Later," with the carefree breeziness that seemed to carry her through every day.

"Lucia, we need to talk."

Nicole seemed to have poofed before me just as I shut my locker.

"Oh, hey," I said, trying to sound like I wasn't alarmed and that I had no idea what she wanted to talk about—what she wanted to *report* on. "Sure, whenever. How about at lunch?"

There was no chatting with Nicole; only interviewing. She had her lavender notepad opened, pen in hand, and she followed me down the halls. Everything that came out of my mouth would now be on the record. I wondered, not for the first time, if Nicole had it out for me. With her last couple of articles I thought her journalism was getting a little yellow, drumming up scandals to sell her stories.

"I'm doing an investigation on the vending machines, Lucia." The word "investigation" unnerved me. No—it downright scared me. "What's going on with them? I heard from maintenance that they haven't been restocked once. Are you aware that the coaches are allegedly selling illegal candy out by their offices? What's your council doing?"

"Look, Nicole," I said, fully realizing I had to carefully choose my words. Even though my mom taught me to never assume anything, I did assume that Nicole was simply investigating the popularity of the vending machines, and not how they got in our halls in the first place. I said, "Why don't you come to our council meeting after school today at five after three? Hear for yourself what we're working on. Sound good?" I glanced down at her Tevas as she jotted this down, wondering if her toes ever got cold.

"Fine. I'll see you then."

As she walked away, I forced myself to take a deep breath. As long as I kept the press on my side, everything would be fine.

★

After school, I headed to Mrs. Peoria's room. I felt the weight of this year's issues—the vending machines, the vote, Ms. Jenkins—and I knew how important this meeting was. It had to go perfectly.

Mrs. Peoria left the moment I walked in the room.

"I'll be in the teacher's lounge if you need anything," she said, carrying a stack of quizzes and a paperback book. The cover was pink, and I wondered if it was a romance novel.

I arranged the desks in a circle like always, adding a fifth so that Nicole could join us. When Cooper arrived he sat down across from me and pulled out a notebook and a pen. I noticed he'd gelled up his hair a little more than usual.

Next Melanie arrived, yawning loudly, her Irish beanie still flopping perfectly to the side despite it being the end of the day. "Hey, guys," she said as she sat down next to Cooper. Nicole followed closely behind her, and Melanie joked, "What up, Nicole? You finally decide to come to the dark side?" I cringed. I didn't want Nicole to think we were not all on the same team. I laughed at Melanie's joke—maybe a bit louder than I should have.

Three ten came and went, and we waited for Jared to arrive, just like we had at the first meeting. I shouldn't have expected him to grace us with his presence—on time, especially—but I tried to stay hopeful. I had texted everyone in the afternoon, reminding them about the meeting and asking them, in a very friendly way, to be on time. Jared finally arrived at three fifteen.

"What'd I miss?" he asked, dropping his bag on the floor by his desk and slumping back in his seat.

"Jared, remember that we discussed tardiness to meetings?" I actually sort of cringed when I heard myself—I sounded like a teacher, and not in a good way. Besides, I was too aware of Nicole watching—and writing down—our every move.

"Oh, I'm aware of the bylaws," he said. My stomach dropped and I waited for him to say more. He spotted Nicole and sneered, "What's she doing here?"

I let out a deep breath, realizing he wasn't going to say more. "Everyone," I began, "Nicole Jeffries, Angus's top reporter, is going to sit through our meeting for a piece she's working on for the school paper. She's just here to observe." I smiled at her to show that everything was cool.

"Don't mind me." She waved.

"Okay, then," I started, clapping my hands together. Cooper uncapped his pen and prepared to take notes. "I hope everyone got a chance to look over the agenda I e-mailed. If you didn't bring a copy, I have some extras here." Only Cooper had brought his, so I handed copies out to Melanie, Jared, and Nicole.

"Item one on the agenda is brainstorming ideas for the new vending machines, how we can help boost sales and really get the word out that they're great and everyone should give them a real chance. Who wants to start?"

The group was silent. Cooper kept his head down, doodling in his notebook. Melanie sat back at her desk, tapping her pirate-topped pencil on her closed biology book. Finally, Jared raised his hand.

"I have an idea. Why don't we get rid of them and bring back the old ones? I don't know anyone who likes those things."

"Thank you, Jared." I wanted to kill him. "But I'd like to keep the discussion positive. The machines have only been out for a few weeks, and I think we need to give everyone some time to get used to them. The food is actually quite good."

I was totally lying, but what was I supposed to say? That I was afraid I'd made a huge mistake that not only cost the school a ton of money, but might even possibly make Ms. Jenkins lose her job? That everyone was wrong and the student council *did* do stuff—bad, horribly wrong stuff?

I didn't think so.

Besides, we had to keep the machines. Ms. Jenkins told me that they had signed a one-year lease on them. If we sent them back, the penalty for breaking the contract would be greater than just sticking it out.

Jared said, "I've tried the food. The thing is, Lucia"—he leaned forward in his seat—"it sucks."

"Again, Jared," I said, "thank you, but I'd really prefer it if we tried to think of solutions instead of just giving up on the machines. What are some ideas to drive business to them? I was thinking of having a contest. Like, we could mark the back of one of the items in the machines, and whoever bought that product would win a prize. Like movie tickets or something."

"Who would pay for the prizes?" Jared asked.

"I was thinking we could probably get one of the local theaters to donate a few tickets. The theater at the mall has done stuff like this before." I looked at Melanie, who was looking at Cooper. "Melanie? Let's hear the ideas you came up with last night."

She snapped her head toward me. "What? Oh." She

dug through her folder and papers. "Um, let me see, I think I wrote something down somewhere."

I clacked my nails on my desk as I watched her dig through her unruly papers while Cooper continued to doodle.

Even though I knew Melanie didn't have any ideas, I said, "Why don't you just tell us your ideas?"

She stopped looking through her papers. She didn't look at me when she said, "I'm sorry. I don't have any."

I let out a deep sigh and instantly regretted it. I looked at Nicole, writing, but she didn't seem to notice.

Jared raised his hand. "Yes?" I asked.

"Why don't we torch them? Collect the insurance?" Melanie stifled a laugh, and I noticed that, even as Nicole took notes, she was also smiling.

"Can we please be serious? This is an important issue."

"Yeah, well, this whole thing is shady if you ask me," Jared said.

"Excuse me?" I asked, but I really didn't want to know. Anyone could tell this was not going to be good.

"The whole voting thing," he explained. "Forcing us to vote without really getting a chance to think it through. It just seems weird, that's all."

I couldn't believe it. Jared was about to out me and I don't think he even knew. Or maybe he did but he wanted to torture me.

Why had I invited Nicole to this meeting?

"I'm sorry, Jared, but I don't have the authority to force any of you to do anything. And we all know you didn't approve the machines. Your voice was heard. But now we're here as a united front to try to improve the situation."

"I'm just saying. The machines were your idea. You fix them." He sat back, apparently having said his piece. I looked at Nicole, who had stopped writing but was taking in the scene.

I felt prickles of angry sweat building under my arms. "Jared," I said, trying so hard to control myself, "this council doesn't honor or condemn one person with an idea. It's a team effort. We speak with one voice. Like when we debuted the machines—we were all there." I looked right at Melanie, who seemed to refuse to return my gaze. "Most of us, anyway."

"Dude, big deal Mel wasn't there," Jared said, and I wondered why he came to her defense so quickly. "We all just stood there doing nothing. What was the point? It was *your* show, and those machines are still a huge failure."

"And that's what we're here to help fix!" I snapped. Realizing I was clenching my pen, I placed it gently on my desk. "Let's e-mail ideas around to each other over the next week. That way you can go home and think about it some more." I looked down at the agenda and decided the rest of it could wait.

I dismissed everyone—Nicole dashed out just behind Jared, and my stomach did an anxious flop when I saw her catch up to him. Was she asking him questions? Did he realize that whatever he said to her when she held that lavender notebook was on the record?

I didn't even notice Melanie leave until I realized Cooper was alone, waiting for me.

"You okay?" he cautiously asked.

I didn't know what to say. I was happy that he was waiting for me and hadn't left with Melanie, but also a little scared, like this meeting had been the beginning of something very, very bad. I thought about telling Cooper what was going on and how scared I was, but I was afraid of how he'd react. I didn't want him to think less of me. I could handle just about anything but that.

"Yes," I said. I forced a smile. "I'm fine."

★

BLUE JAYS . . .
THE VIEW FROM ABOVE

Special Investigation:

Latham Exposed

BY NICOLE JEFFRIES

Could lies and deception be behind the success of our school's only three-peat student council president, Lucia Latham? After extensive research and exclusive interviews, this reporter has learned that this may be the case.

Ms. Latham herself extended an invitation to her latest student council meeting. On the agenda: boosting sales of the new vending machines. As many Blue Jays may be unaware, these vending machines, which can often be seen covered in biohazard tape and not being used by the student body, are the brainchild of Ms. Latham, and Ms. Latham alone. But what's more shocking is that our president has used illegal voting tactics to push her agenda through the unsuspecting council.

In an exclusive interview with student council treasurer Jared Hensley, he says, "I thought it was kind of weird when Lucia asked us to vote on these machines at the very first meeting, which wasn't even supposed to be our first meeting. She called us in before the preplanned meeting that was scheduled in my student council welcome packet. Anyway, that's when she first told us about the machines." He went on to say, "When she said we had to vote by midnight that same night, I thought that seemed kind of quick. Especially since she'd given us, like, twenty pages of info to read."

Indeed, Mr. Hensley's instinct was correct. Article VI, Section 2, of the Angus Junior High Student Council Bylaws reads that "any council vote in which money is involved must have a one-week (seven days) research period between presentation of item and vote. Approval is at the discretion of the principal."

Further complicating matters is the fact that Ms. Latham called the meeting at all, as it was not, as Mr. Hensley stated, a preconfirmed meeting.

Ms. Jenkins confirmed that she approved the vending machines, but seemed aware of the mandatory review time.

When Vice President Melanie O'Hare was approached about this matter, she very tellingly answered, "Yeah, we voted fast, whatever. If Lucia thought the machines were a good idea, then I'm behind her." When asked if she thought the food was any good, Ms. O'Hare suddenly dashed off to class.

When Ms. Latham herself was asked about the matter, she became visibly frustrated and would only say, "I do not recall." But a simple review of the first meeting's minutes shows that she did, indeed, blatantly ignore the rules. When asked about the matter, Student Council Adviser Mrs. Peoria curtly replied, "No comment!" As this reporter knows, "no comment" speaks volumes.

The bylaws are clear on this matter. If Ms. Latham forced the rules in her favor on this project, should Blue Jays worry about what else she's done—or what else she could do?

★★★★★ **14** ★★★★★

When the school paper came out two days after the meeting, I snatched a copy, ran to a corner in a empty hallway, and read the article. I felt like the story couldn't possibly be about me. I could hardly make out the words, my eyes zipped so quickly across the page. At the time, the only thoughts I could process were, *Is this person me? Am I really this sneaky and controlling?*

I shoved the paper into my backpack and rolled it down the hallway, trying to comprehend what was happening. Then I heard my name being called.

"Lucia!" called Mrs. Peoria. "My classroom, now."

I could barely handle the weight of my backpack as I dragged my feet to her classroom.

"Shut the door," she instructed. "Now, sit down." I sat front and center, mentally preparing myself for whatever was about to happen.

Mrs. Peoria began by saying, "Do I look like an idiot to you?" My throat was so dry I couldn't even get a squeak out, so I just shook my head, no. "Because, young lady, I feel that you have made me look like an idiot." She held the paper in front of me. "Is this true?" I nodded my head, yes. "I give you the freedom to hold your meetings without my supervision, and this is the thanks I get?" She tossed the paper onto her desk. I had to admit I'd never seen her this animated before. There was life inside Mrs. P after all. "I've called your parents to inform them about this, and I've scheduled a meeting with Ms. Jenkins to decide how we're going to handle this." She paused for a moment, then said, "I have to admit, Lucia, I didn't think you had this in you. I'm very disappointed."

When she dismissed me, I practically sprinted out of school, which had mostly cleared out by then. I missed the bus home but I didn't care. I was too ashamed to face anyone. No one had ever yelled at me before—I was a good person and always did as I was told—and having Mrs. Peoria so mad at me made me feel ashamed. I didn't want to disappoint anyone, including myself. But it seemed that's exactly what I had done.

I knew I had to call my dad to come get me, and

I wondered if Mrs. Peoria called him or Mom. If she called Dad, I might be able to convince him to stay quiet on this and avoid massive punishment from Mom.

When he pulled up, I rolled my backpack down to his Camry; I could see him smiling before I even opened the door, so I knew he hadn't gotten the call. Even though there was no way he could know what was happening, his seemingly carefree manner bugged me.

"What happened?" Dad asked as we pulled away from the school.

"I missed the bus."

"One of your important business meetings run late?"

"Yeah." I don't know what, other than my own misery, made me say, "Remember those?"

"Lord, Lucia." Dad sighed, his good mood gone just like that. My shame and embarrassment had turned me mean and nasty, even though I knew Dad was just being friendly. All I could think about was what was going to happen when Mom got home.

I stared out the window, watching the houses go by, wondering what was going on inside each of them. "You just, you have no idea," Dad muttered, shaking his head. "Listen, there's something I want to talk to you about. Something I want to say." I kept my gaze out the window. "I know you don't understand why I'm not work-ing. It's adult stuff that's hard to explain. I was a boxer for ten years; then I became an accountant. Now, I'm nei-ther. And I don't know what I'm supposed to do with myself anymore—even what I want to do."

"How about look for a job?" I said. I figured things couldn't get any worse, so why not be a smart-mouth? But Dad just sighed.

"Don't assume you know everything."

The thing is, I used to look up to my dad. I used to rely on him to show me how to be tough, mentally and physically. When he taught me how to take a punch in sixth grade against a kid my size at the boxing gym (Mom never heard about this—she would have killed us both), it wasn't just to show me how it hurt my body. He did it to show how it hurt my pride, and how to fight back from that. "Fighting isn't always about throwing punches," he'd said. "Sometimes it's about avoiding them."

I shifted in my seat to face him and said, "There's this quote from the movie *Million Dollar Baby* where the guy says, 'Sometimes, the best way to deliver a punch is to step back. But step back too far, and you're not fighting at all.' Dad, that's what you're doing. How come?"

In the weary smile that etched its way across his lips, I could see my comment made him happy and a bit sad—maybe for his old life at the gym. "It's different now. Harder, I guess." He paused. "Who'd want to hire an old guy like me when they can get college graduates cheaper?"

He'd never talked to me like that before. It was a little weird, but I liked that he felt I could handle it. Also, it felt really good talking about something totally unrelated to school. "Don't think so low of yourself, Dad. You have to at least try."

He rolled his lips in, keeping his eyes on the road. Almost to himself, he whispered, "I know."

At home, we found Mom waiting in the kitchen looking about as angry as I'd ever seen her.

"Everything okay?" Dad asked as he dropped his keys on the kitchen counter.

She didn't even look at him—only me. "I got a call at work this afternoon from Mrs. Peoria." My stomach sank. I couldn't even look at her. "Now, I just want to hear the truth, because I know what she's saying isn't true."

"What's going on?" Dad asked. I tried to find the ability to speak.

"William, not now," Mom said to him, as if the matter didn't concern him.

"Excuse me," he said, raising his voice, "but she's my daughter too."

Mom closed her eyes and put a hand on her hip—always a bad sign. "Mrs. Peoria called to tell me that my daughter has cheated to get her way at school, and I am sure I raised you better than to do something so cheap and despicable."

"What'd she do?" Dad asked.

As I was still unable to speak, Mom spoke up for me. She was talking to Dad but kept her eyes on me. "She forced a student council vote to get her own way. Isn't that true, Lucia?"

Dad looked at me but said nothing.

Finally, I squeaked out to Mom, "Well, sort of. Not really."

"Not really?" Mom snapped. "Then *what*, really?"

I couldn't look her in the eyes. I couldn't look Dad in the eyes either. I could feel their disappointment all around me, like a too-hot blanket.

Mom's voice became calm. She crossed her arms over her stomach and looked up to the ceiling. "So this is how

I raised my daughter. Get to your room," she snapped.

I turned on my heel and ran to my room before the tears could spill down my face.

I couldn't believe myself. I'd been so desperate to make a huge, positive change in my last year as president that I had lost my focus and basically cheated. And worse, not only had I disappointed Mrs. Peoria, whose opinion I hadn't realized I cared about, and my dad, but I had disappointed my mom to the point that she couldn't even look at me.

I buried my face in my pillows, clutching Paddy close to me, and cried—actually, more like bawled. I could feel the veins in my neck bulging. I got it all out, hard, efficiently, in five minutes. Then I sat up, wiped my face, and wondered what was going to happen to me at school the next day. I wasn't sure how the whole thing would play out, or what Ms. Jenkins would do once everyone read the paper.

Which made me think of the online polls.

I told myself not to do it even as I turned on my computer. I wondered how the poll would be worded, and how bad the numbers would be stacked against me. As I logged on to our school's site, I was not prepared for just how bad it would be.

As reported exclusively by Nicole Jeffries, Lucia Latham cheated the student council vote to get the unpopular healthy vending machines installed. Do you think she should step down from office for her blatant disregard for the law?
- No, the rule she broke isn't that big of a deal.
- Yes, if she lies and cheats on this, what else might she do?

My hand shook over the mouse as I viewed the poll results: 85 percent for stepping down.

I tossed Paddy to the floor, and for the first time in my life, I sneaked out of my room.

As I ran to Cooper's house, I thought of what boxing meant to me. It was about endurance. You feel like you want to collapse at the end of each round, like you don't have any more strength left in you, but you have to keep going. Once you're in that ring, there isn't any other choice. And that's what I would do too. Unlike Dad, I wouldn't quit. I would endure.

I felt slightly better as I walked up Cooper's driveway. I was already getting stronger, or at least telling myself to have more confidence.

I could see that their garage door, which was on the

side of the house, was open and the lights were on. I could hear Cooper saying, "That's it. Good!" I heard that familiar smacking of gloves.

When the inside of the garage came into view, I saw Cooper wearing the yellow focus mitts we sometimes used for target practice. I stood immobile outside the garage. He stopped the second he saw me, and got clocked in the mitt by the other person's pink glove. When the person turned to look at me, I saw that it was Melanie. Boxing with Cooper. In my gear.

I could hardly speak. I couldn't believe what I was seeing. Boxing was *our* thing. It wasn't hers. It was just another whim that she'd forget about in three days, just like everything else. And because I couldn't think of anything to say, I looked at Melanie and yelled, "You said you were Irish!" then turned around and ran back home.

★ ★ ★ ★ ★ **15** ★ ★ ★ ★ ★

Mom drove me to school the next morning even though she was barely talking to me. I couldn't bear facing Melanie—or anyone else—on the bus.

I was angry with Melanie and the boxing, and angry with myself for what I had done at school. As I walked the halls I kept my chin up—to show the school (or maybe myself) that I would endure. I just knew I had to be brave. Before I would let myself really process or deal with Melanie, I knew I had to apologize for the vote.

Jared was the first council member I saw. He was leaning against the lockers before first period, talking to April DeHart, a perky cheerleader who was always on the top of the pyramids. I was surprised she was giving Jared the time of day, but she giggled as he spoke, her round cheeks glowing pink.

"Hey, Jared," I said as I approached them. I told myself

that he would be the most difficult to talk to, and once I explained myself to him, the others would come more easily.

When Jared looked at me, the smile fell from his face. Even April stiffened.

"Can I talk to you for a second? Alone?" I looked to April and tried to give her a look that said, *You understand, don't you?* She glared back at me.

Jared looked down at the carpet. "I'm not sure I'm ready to talk to you, Latham. I feel very deceived right now."

"I know, but look," I said, "it'll only take a sec. Please?"

"Fine," he said. "Say what you want, but say it here." April stood up straighter, as if to protect Jared from my evilness.

I told myself that others *should* hear what I had to say; I *wanted* everyone to know that I understood what a huge, stupid mistake I had made. I squared my shoulders and said, "Okay. Well, I just wanted to say that I'm really sorry for not following the rules. I just wanted to get the vending machines vote through because Ms. Jenkins wanted it on the school board agenda, and I didn't think it was a big deal. But now I know it was."

Jared looked up at me, his brows pulled together. "So, what? You only did it because Ms. Jenkins made you?"

"No, that's not what I meant. She wanted it on the next meeting agenda, but—"

"Dang, Latham. You're unbelievable. How about taking some responsibility?"

"Yeah," April squeaked, but I barely paid her any attention because that was not what I meant to say.

"Ms. Jenkins rocks," Jared said, "and I, for one, won't let you blame your own sneaky ways on her."

"No, that's not what I meant. And I didn't mean to be sneaky."

Jared snorted, and April linked her arm through his. "Come on, Jared," she said in a soft voice as she glared at me. "Let's get out of here."

"I just wanted to do something nice for the school," I tried.

I stared at them as they walked away and heard students *tsk* me as they headed to class. I felt like crying, and I'd never hated myself more than I did just then.

In the halls, people gave me dirty looks. Even Lily Schmidt, who was finding her voice more and more, managed to snip to me in algebra, "You shouldn't have cheated."

When I got to the cafeteria, I saw Cooper. His shirt was half tucked in, like maybe he was making an effort of some sort. He was with Max, but I barely saw him, even though I think he said hello to me. Cooper told him he'd see him inside, and Max hesitated for a moment before telling Cooper he'd save him a seat.

Seeing Cooper gave me this weird mix of feelings I'd never had with him. Massive confusion, if that's an actual feeling, was the strongest.

We stood before the Naturally Natural vending machine—the same one I had inaugurated just a few weeks ago. There were still pieces of a skull-and-bones picture that hadn't been torn down completely on the side of it. I picked at them while Cooper waited for me to say something.

"Hey," I finally said.

"Hey," he replied.

We didn't speak for several excruciating moments. I didn't know what I was supposed to say, and I guess he didn't either. Avoiding what I really wanted to ask him ("Do you like her?!"), I said, "So, I guess you saw the paper?"

He looked me right in the eyes and said, "I understand why you did it. I mean, you didn't have to, and

I don't think any less of you for it. You know," he said, "Nicole had me turn over my meeting notes to her. She cited some Freedom of Information Act or something." It was the very act I helped implement two years ago. "They're being really hard on you, Loosh. I don't think it's fair."

I managed a smile. "Thanks, but I think it's exactly fair."

"If you want me to talk to anyone—Nicole or Mrs. Peoria—just say the word. I'll do anything."

I let that last sentence linger in my head a moment. *I'll do anything.* Cooper was the most solid thing in my life, and I didn't want anything between us to change—not ever. "Thanks," I finally managed, feeling tears sting the corners of my eyes. I kept my eyes on my shoes.

We stood for a moment until finally he said, "I shouldn't have let Melanie use your gloves without asking you. I'm sorry."

I didn't look at Cooper when I said, "No biggie. I shouldn't have kept the research period thing secret."

"No biggie," he replied.

I wanted to ask him if Melanie was any good at boxing, if it would be a regular thing, and just how much time were they spending together? I also wanted to scream, *Don't ever do it again!* but I guess I showed a rare moment of restraint.

He motioned to the cafeteria. "You going in?"

I had my lunch with me, and even though I had walked to the caf with every intention of going in and eating, suddenly I didn't feel like it. Even though seeing Cooper made me feel better, it also made me feel horrible. If that makes any sense. "I think I'm just gonna walk around for a bit."

He nodded like he understood. "I'll be around," he said.

Leaving the cafeteria, I put my hands into the pockets of my black pants, which were getting a little short in the hem, and stormed across the windy athletic field, then banged on the temporary building's door before opening it myself.

Coach Fleck looked up from his metal desk. "Well, hey there, Prez."

"Hi."

"What brings you out to these parts? Don't tell me there's been more budget cuts and you're taking away our offices." He laughed at that, and so did Coach Ryan, who was on the other side of the office, at his own desk.

I jerked my head toward the vending machine

crammed against the wall. "Gimme the chocolate doughnuts and a Coke." I pulled some money out of my pocket and offered it to him.

He let out a long whistle. "Must be a rough day," he said, getting up to get me the loot. Handing it over he said, "First one's on the house, kid." I snatched it out of his hands and quickly left, shutting the door on their laughter.

I scarfed the doughnuts and guzzled half the Coke just walking across the field. I buried the evidence in the trashcan outside the cafeteria, hoping Lori Anne wasn't lurking around the corner like a paparazzo, snapping incriminating pictures. Before I could even decide where to go next or what to do, I ran into Melanie. My stomach, which was already dangling somewhere around my knees, plummeted to the floor.

"Oh, hey," I said. Melanie looked as cute as ever in a gray fedora with a red feather that matched the belt on her white blouse. She was with Rose Andreas, who wore a long tangle of pink opaque stones around her neck, and Catherine Collins, who darted her eyes nervously from me to Melanie. "You guys go ahead, I'll be there in a sec," Melanie told them. When they left, she said, "I've been looking for you."

I could barely look at her but saw that she was watching me closely, carefully.

"How are you holding up?" she asked. "You okay?"

I shrugged like it was no big thing. "I'm fine." Even though I was mad at her for boxing with Cooper—*in my gear*—I really wanted to apologize about the voting thing, because I honestly felt awful about it. "I'm really sorry about not telling you about the research period with the voting."

For a second Melanie looked like she didn't know what I was talking about. Then she said, "Oh, that? I could care less."

When I didn't say more, she asked, "Hey, are you mad at me?"

"No," I lied.

"Because I was sort of worried that you would be, about the boxing thing."

"Nuh-uh." I didn't even try to sound reassuring. I didn't have the energy.

"It's just that, you made boxing seem so cool and all, and like a great workout, and I wanted to try it. And Cooper said you wouldn't mind if I used your gloves and stuff."

I hated thinking about her wearing my gloves,

playing my sport, with my best friend. I wanted to know if Cooper was just her latest fad, one she'd abandon in two weeks, and if so, I'd have to immediately whoop her for it. But I didn't say any of that to her. "It's fine. I don't care."

"Okay," she said, somewhat carefully. "Are you going in to lunch?"

"No, I'm going for a walk around the field," I said.

Melanie nodded. "Okay. Well, I'll see you on the bus, right?"

"Yeah, I'll be there."

"Cool. Take it easy, Lucia."

I turned to walk toward the field, but before I could get too far, a thought sprang into my head like a Mexican jumping bean. "Wait! Melanie!"

She turned to me, the brim of her fedora shading her left eye. "Yeah?"

"Did Cooper wrap your hands?" She looked at me questioningly. "You know, with the black cloth wrap? Before you put on the gloves?"

"No," she said. "I just wore the gloves. Why?"

Feeling mildly relieved, I said, "No reason," then walked away.

By the end of lunch, everyone had read the article and most had seen the online poll. By the end of the day, the school was calling for my resignation.

I got a note in last-period physical science. I expected it to be from Ms. Jenkins, and it was. She wanted to see me immediately after the bell.

When I walked into her office, she tossed her pen, sat back, and folded her arms.

"I know." I sighed as I sat down. "I messed up." I didn't want Ms. Jenkins, who (along with my mom) was probably already disappointed in me, to hate me or think I was a sneaky little jerk.

"Lucia," she began, shaking her head. Her face and voice softened, and she said, "Honey, what were you thinking?"

Feeling better that she spoke to me so gently, I said,

"I guess I wasn't. The only thing on my mind was making sure the vote went through in time."

"I feel like," she began, "you took advantage of the council's not knowing the bylaws." I felt tears well up when she said that. "Now, I'm not saying I'm blameless. I should have known those laws better. That was my mistake. And I take responsibility for asking you to get it done so quickly. For that I apologize."

I blinked my eyes fast to keep the tears from falling. "What should I do?" I asked miserably.

"Well, start with Nicole. Go on record with your apology. Look," she said, leaning forward on her desk. "If you're really sorry about what you did, and you truly didn't mean any kind of malice or trickery, then people will forgive you. If they believe you, they'll forgive you."

I nodded. Ms. Jenkins always expected more from me than from the other students, and I appreciated that. And to be honest, I was pretty scared about how I'd gotten myself into this situation, but I knew that a big part of boxing was controlling your fears—namely, the fear of getting the crap beat out of you—and doing it with dignity. I really was sorry for not telling the whole truth to the council, and I needed to make sure everyone else knew that. I owed that not just to the council, but to the whole school.

When I left Ms. Jenkins's office, I realized that I had, once again, missed the school bus. Dad arrived ten minutes after I called him.

"Should we make this a regular date?" he asked as I pulled on my seat belt.

I couldn't even respond, the knot in my throat was so tight. I'd developed a killer headache as soon as I left Ms. Jenkins's office, and I just wanted to go home and have a moment of peace before I plunged feetfirst into figuring out how I would fix the mess I had created.

Later that night in my room, I dug out my secret stash of corn chips, eating with salty, oily fingers as I pondered the benefits of a public castigation. I finished off the whole bag, which called itself "snack size" but had about the entire daily allowance of calories. I heard the front doorbell ring as I slid my finger around the inside of the empty bag, then Dad calling my name. I licked my fingers and came to the door to find Cooper and Melanie.

"Hi," Cooper said, and I could tell he was treading lightly. I guess that's what you do to a person who might break down or explode at any moment. "You busy?"

"I'm just trying to figure out what I'm going to do about everything."

"Yeah," Cooper said, "we figured."

"That's why we're here," Melanie said brightly. "To rescue you."

I looked to Cooper. "We know you're stressed," he explained. "And we think everyone's being so harsh on you."

"Way harsh, Loosh," Melanie added.

"And we knew you were probably sitting in your bedroom—"

"Stressing," Melanie said.

"So we thought we'd come get you out of the house for a little while so you could clear your head."

They looked at me hopefully. "You guys sure have banded together," I noted.

"For you!" cheered Melanie.

"We promise we won't keep you out long," Cooper said.

I stood in the doorway for a moment. "Okay." I grabbed my jacket from the hall closet, feeling only slightly better. "Where're we going?"

We walked to the elementary school a few blocks away. Every time we passed beneath a streetlight, I could see my breath in the cold night air. I wished I had brought my gloves.

The elementary school got a new playground last year, and it has swings that go really high. Even though we knew it was sort of babyish, there was no denying that it was fun to act like a kid sometimes.

We raced each other to the giant swing set and jumped into the seats—me, Melanie, then Cooper.

"Whoever gets the highest first, wins!" called Melanie as we all kicked off.

As we pulled ourselves higher, the cold air whooshed across my cheeks and fluttered my bangs off my forehead. I leaned far back in the seat, my hands wrapped around the cold chains, and pushed my feet out in front of me as I worked to gain more height. Nothing was so bad that I couldn't fix it, I told myself as Melanie and I passed each other, each going in exactly opposite directions.

"See?" she called as we passed each other. "Fun!"

Cooper, who swung in unison with Melanie, his baggy shirt fluttering behind him like a cape, pointed across the playground and yelled, "Seesaw!"

"Yes!" she said. "Let's make a jump for it."

"Higher first!" hollered Cooper.

Still perfectly in sync, they counted to three, then flew out of their swings like stuntmen. Melanie dashed across the patchy grass with Cooper just behind her.

As they hopped onto the seesaw, I dragged my feet to a stop in the gravel. I couldn't hear them, but Cooper said something that made Melanie throw back her head and laugh, causing her to almost lose her hat.

I walked toward them. I sat on a chipmunk spring rider and gave it a little rock. Watching my two best friends, I finally realized that they had something that didn't include me. I always thought that I was the one that held us all together, but then I realized that maybe they didn't need me after all. Seeing them together, having so much fun, made me wish they'd never tried to cheer me up in the first place.

★ ★ ★ ★ ★ **17** ★ ★ ★ ★ ★

By the time I woke up the next morning, I was ready to announce my mistake and apologize to the whole school. Talking to Nicole was first on my list.

"Nicole," I said to her between classes, "I'd like to talk to you on record about that vote."

I thought there'd be a spark of excitement in her eyes about getting this scoop, but as usual, she looked unfazed. I guess as a reporter you had to stay even. "Caf at lunch?"

"How about on the edge of the athletic fields?"

"Fine."

I'd ridden the bus to school that morning. I sat with Melanie, but something was different. I don't know if it was her or me, but there was tension in us both, and our conversation felt forced. I didn't mention the playground, and she didn't offer any insight into her and Cooper's budding (blossomed?) love affair.

While I waited for Nicole, I nibbled on some Cheese Nips I had in my coat pocket. When I saw her coming— still wearing those Tevas, even though it was freezing and the socks couldn't be helping *that* much—I tried to wipe the crumbs off my fingers on the inside of my pocket. The headache I'd been nursing pounded with new strength, and I wondered if it was from all the junk food that I'd been gorging on.

"Thanks for meeting me," I said as Nicole and I sat down.

She took a tape recorder out of her bag and set it on the grass between us, then pushed the record button. With the red light glowing, she said, "All right. So, what've you got?"

I took a deep breath. I hadn't expected to be so nervous. "Well, uh, I just want you, and everyone else at this school, especially the other members of the student council, to know how sorry I am about the vote. It's true, I did know the research-period rule of seven days before casting a major vote, and I said nothing when I asked my council for a quick vote. So for that, I'm really sorry."

"Fine," Nicole said. "What else?"

What else? I wasn't sure what else I was expected to

do, so I said, "Just, you know, I'm really sorry. It won't happen again."

"It shouldn't have happened in the first place," Nicole said.

"I know," I agreed. "But it was a onetime lie. Not even a lie. A not-tell. And it won't happen again."

"Uh-huh," Nicole muttered, as if she didn't quite believe this. "Will you step down from your presidency if the school demands it?"

I paused. I meant it when I said I was sorry, but I also felt the student body would understand that I'd made a mistake, that I was trying to fix it, and then everything would go back to being okay. They'd never paid me much attention before, so now I was sort of hoping they'd keep not doing what they hadn't been doing all along.

"I'm confident that the students will accept my honest apology, and that it won't come to that," I said.

"If you are forced down," Nicole persisted, "what kind of president do you think Melanie O'Hare will be?"

I felt a tightness in my chest, and the pounding in my head intensified. I didn't want to hear about Melanie as president or any sort of resignation of mine. I tried to unclench my jaw as I said, "She's not even an issue because I won't be stepping down."

"So, you don't think the school will force you down?"

"Like I said, Nicole," I said slowly, "I have every confidence that—"

"Lucia, everyone's angry." Nicole's tone turned; it was more forceful, yet with a measure of pleading, like she really wanted me to listen. "You understand that, right? They don't trust you. In the halls, people are saying it's not fair that you get to bend the rules when no one else does. It's like," she said, "cheating on a test. If you cheat on a test, you get a zero plus detention. But you cheated on something major, and people think you should be punished."

I rubbed the back of my neck, trying to process what she was saying, feeling desperate. "I just . . . I'm really sorry. I think I deserve a second chance. I hope that people will—"

"Are you saying you wouldn't step down even if called to?" Nicole interrupted.

I couldn't believe it. She was serious. After all the hard work I'd done for the student body, and after years of getting zero recognition for trying to do good stuff, they only took notice when I'd done something wrong.

"No one is calling for me to step down," I said, working overtime to keep my panic in check.

Nicole looked me dead in the eyes. "But they are."

I stared back at her. "If it comes to that, I'll do the right thing."

I tried to use the rest of my time with Nicole in a grasping-at-straws attempt to encourage people to use the vending machines. She finally cut me off and said she needed to get back to the newsroom, which was actually just Mrs. Troxel's classroom, and transcribe the interview.

But it turns out I didn't even need the interview with Nicole to redeem myself. I got a note in seventh-period physical science to go to Ms. Jenkins's office—stat. As I approached the administrative offices, I saw Melanie coming out, but she turned in the opposite direction before she saw me.

I walked into Ms. Jenkins's office and found she had company. Mrs. Peoria sat in my usual chair, pushing back her cuticles. Beside her sat Mrs. Lack, our school counselor, her hands folded in her lap and a look of overstated concern on her small face.

"Have a seat, Lucia," Ms. Jenkins said. She didn't look at me.

My legs shook as I sat in the extra chair that had been brought in, next to Mrs. Peoria. She didn't acknowledge me, but she did stop bothering with her cuticles.

"I'm sure you know why we've brought you in," Ms. Jenkins said. I tried to swallow. "Lucia, I know that it may seem that what you did isn't that big of a deal, but I'm afraid it is. After looking more carefully at the bylaws, I'm afraid I can't let something like this be glossed over."

"I talked to Nicole Jeffries," I told her. "I did what you told me to do—I fixed it. I apologized to everyone. The article comes out first thing next week."

Ms. Jenkins looked at me sadly. "I'm afraid it's too late."

"But I said I was sorry. I acknowledged my mistake."

"Lucia, I'm sorry." Her brows were furrowed in a pain-filled scrunch. "I don't want to do this. As president, you're in a position of trust."

"I went to everyone individually and apologized," I quickly said.

"Not the trust of just your student council," she said gently, "but of your entire class. This is about more than just your friends forgiving you. You do understand that, don't you?" Her watery eyes looked between me and Mrs. Lack, as if looking for guidance, or a way out. "Lucia, you know how much I admire you. And I feel awful for my part in this. That's why I'm giving you the chance to resign. Otherwise, we'll have to impeach you."

My heart dropped. Impeach me? I never thought I'd hear those words spoken about me. Impeachment meant having the student council vote on whether or not I got to stay in office. If I'd been thinking clearly, I might have taken my chances with their vote. Cooper would never vote me out, Jared probably would, and I was pretty sure Melanie would never do that. But right then my mind was so scrambled that I couldn't think straight. Talk about needing time to think it over.

"I can accept your resignation right now," Ms. Jenkins said. "Mrs. Peoria and I can."

No, I wanted to say. *I don't want to resign. I shouldn't have to resign*. Why were they doing this to me? The students had never liked me, even though they'd voted me in, and they'd been waiting for a chance to take me down. Which, I guess, is why I said what I said next to Ms. Jenkins.

"I don't want to be impeached," I said, a huge sob building in the back of my throat. "It's not fair," I cried like a big baby.

"Can you give us a moment?" Ms. Jenkins said to Mrs. Lack and Mrs. Peoria as I began a full-on crying fit. Once they had shut the door behind them, Ms. Jenkins said, "Lucia. Honey." She handed me a tissue, and I blew my nose, trying to pull myself together. "I see a lot of myself in you. Did you know that I am this school district's youngest principal?"

"Of course," I said through great gulps of air.

"I know this is hard," she said. "But in politics—in life sometimes—you have to be firm, even when being firm doesn't seem fair. You did do the right thing by apologizing immediately, and I'm glad you spoke to your council directly. In fact, I'm having to do the same thing right now to the school board about the vending machines. They're questioning the whole thing. . . ."

"The sales are getting better! They will!"

"Lucia." She looked at me sadly, like when you have the unfortunate luck to watch an animal die but there's nothing you can do to save it. "Listen to me carefully: Those vending machines are not your fault. I made the decision to move forward with them. Don't take this the wrong way, but you don't have that much power." She was trying to be funny. I wiped my nose.

"I don't want to be impeached," I said. I wasn't totally sure, but in my mind, right then, I knew that I'd rather resign than be impeached, even if my impeachment didn't result in being kicked off the council. I wiped my eyes and blew my nose one final time. "I'll leave. I'll resign."

With that, I stood up and left Ms. Jenkins's office as she called my name. I didn't want to look at the faux-sympathetic faces of Mrs. Lack and Mrs. Peoria. I was no longer president of the Angus Junior High student council, and that was all that mattered. The count was over, and I was out.

"Attention, Angus Blue Jays, for a late-day announcement." Mrs. Peoria's voice came over the loudspeakers before I could get back to my class. "Please note that effective immediately, Melanie O'Hare will be stepping up as student council president. Have a good weekend."

I didn't want to go back to class. I didn't want to go to my locker, and I didn't want to take the bus home. After hearing the announcement, I just wanted out, but I'd never skipped a class in my life and I wasn't about to start now, even though *now* seemed like the best time to do it. I forced myself to go to class, never once looking anyone in the eyes even though I could feel them all staring at me. When the final bell rang, I walked out of the school and all the way home. Halfway home I just wanted to call Dad and have him come pick me up, but Mom had recently taken away my cell phone, saying it wasn't a necessary expense. So I kept walking.

When I finally got to my room, I pulled the covers over my head, Paddy close at my side, and the promise of a pint of whatever was the most fattening and bad-for-you ice cream waiting for me in the freezer.

I tried to understand how I'd let this happen to me. And then I realized that I had asked for it by wanting it too badly. I had let my emotions get in the way of my rational mind. I was like Mike Tyson when he bit off part of Evander Holyfield's ear when he was losing their huge rematch. Or worse, I was like Prince Naseem Hamed, the arrogant, showboating British fighter who had no problem tackling fighters to the mat when things weren't going his way. I guess that's who I'd turned out to be. Cheating when I wanted my way instead of figuring out the proper way to handle things. And all for health-food vending machines that no one liked anyway.

18

I didn't stay in bed long. My mind couldn't stop working over what had happened, so I got up and went to the
kitchen. No surprise we had no ice cream—that was now
a luxury in our house—but I did find a box of cookies
way in the back of the cupboard that had an expiration
date of two years from now, obviously loaded with pre-
servatives. I realized that even my own family was stashing
junk food, much like Coaches Fleck and Ryan at school.

As I worked on my third cookie, Dad walked into
the kitchen.

"Oh, I didn't hear you come in." He wore jeans with
holes in the knees and an Austin City Limits T-shirt.
"You have an okay day?"

I almost sputtered out my cookie in a sarcastic laugh.
I went to the refrigerator and found a can of Dr Pepper,
which I cracked open and gulped.

"That bad?" Dad asked.

Dragging my feet back to the cookies, I said, "I'm no longer president."

Dad let out a little laugh. Then, realizing I wasn't joking, he said, "No. Seriously?" I nodded as I shoved a whole cookie into my mouth. I felt nauseous, but I didn't care. "What happened?"

Spitting crumbs, I said, "I cheated a vote. I'm out. Ms. Jenkins told me I had to either quit or get kicked out." I knew this wasn't entirely true, but just then the details didn't seem to matter.

"Lord, honey." He ran a hand through his hair. "When did it happen?"

"Seventh period."

"Huh," he said. "Just like me." I looked at him, and he gave me a sheepish look. "When people are let go, they usually do it late in the day on Fridays. Causes less commotion, they say."

This angered me, his comparing my being forced out to his getting sacked. I had worked hard to save my job while he had sat back and watched his get taken away. "Nothing about this is *standard*," I said. Unable to control my temper any longer, I said, "So what did you do today?"

"Not much," he said.

He was about to say more, but I yelled, "Surprise, sur-prise!" and grabbed the rest of the cookies and stormed off to my room, slamming my door.

Later, after having cried so hard that my head pounded with the effort, I thought of going to the school's web-site to see what was written about me in the polls. Only, I wasn't sure I could handle it right then.

Instead I went to Henry's room. There was always an aura of calmness in there, and it smelled good too, espe-cially considering he's a ten-year-old boy. I figured it was just what I needed when I had nowhere else to turn.

"Can I come in?" I asked.

Henry sat on the floor, leaning against his bed and writing in a journal. "Sure," he said.

"What are you doing?" I said, sitting across from him.

"Homework."

"On a Friday night? Even you're not that big of a dork."

Henry shrugged, like maybe he was. "We have to write about a significant moment in our lives."

"You're in fifth grade," I said. "What's happened to you that's significant?"

"I'm writing about Dad."

"Oh," I said. "I already yelled at him today."

"You shouldn't be too hard on him," Henry said. "He just needs to find his center again."

I looked at my younger brother with a bit of awe and admiration. "You never get stressed," I said.

"You're always stressed."

I smiled and nodded. "Maybe I should try some of your meditating stuff."

"You should!" he said, brightening. He tossed his journal aside. "I can teach you how. It'll be so good for you."

Before I could protest, Henry lit a candle, which smelled like sage, and put in his white noise CD. He showed me how to sit with my legs crossed and guided me in a quiet, calm voice.

"Empty your mind of all thoughts," he said. "Visualize your breath going into your lungs . . . relax every muscle in your body . . . feel the worries slide out through your pores. . . ."

I tried to concentrate, but all I could think was, *Don't think, don't think . . . Hey! You're not thinking! Oh, shoot, now you are. . . .* The longer we sat, the more fidgety I became, until Henry finally stated, in his regular voice, "You stink at this."

I started laughing immediately. "Seriously," I said. "It's making me feel more pent up and anxious."

"I don't know why I'm trying to get you to do this. You already have your own way of destressing. Why don't you go down to the Nixons' and box?"

I hadn't even spoken to Cooper—or, for that matter, to Melanie—yet today. I was sure if I went down there and told him I wasn't ready to talk about the student council but that I just needed to box, he would understand. "Good idea," I said, getting up from the floor. "Tell Mom and Dad I'll be back in, like, an hour."

I changed clothes and grabbed my gear, which Cooper had left on our back porch after I'd caught him with Melanie. As I walked down to his house, I realized how strange it was that he hadn't called me first thing after school. What happened to his and Melanie's cheer-up committee, now that things were at their worst?

Cooper answered the door. He seemed to wince when he saw that it was me.

"So," I said, spreading my arms. "Here I am. Angus's first chucked president."

"I meant to call you," he said. "That was so harsh, the announcement they made. Did they tell you they were doing it?"

I let myself in, nudging past him. I stopped just inside the door and turned back to him. "What's that smell? You wearing cologne or something?"

He turned pink as he shut the door. "So, are you okay?"

"No," I said, walking into his living room, where Mrs. Nixon called hello to me from the couch. "I'm not. I really, really need to box now. So go change—and please rinse off some of that *ick* smell."

"You about ready, Coop?" Mr. Nixon emerged from his bedroom. He paused when he saw me, then said hello.

I looked to Cooper, who was turning a darker shade of pink. "Why is your shirt tucked in? And you're wearing a belt."

"We're going to a Rangers game," he said. "The beer guy from Dad's restaurant hooked him up with box seats."

Right on cue, Mrs. Nixon stood up and said, "Is Melanie coming up here, or are we picking her up on the way?"

Now it was my turn to flush, although I'm pretty sure it was a deep, angry shade of red. "Melanie?" I spat. I couldn't help myself. "You're taking Melanie to a baseball game?" I couldn't believe it. First my presidency, now my best friend? She was taking everything from me.

Cooper shrugged, not looking at me.

"On a Friday night, with your parents? What is this, a double date or something?" Cooper's face tensed up, and

Mr. Nixon said, "Son, we'll wait for you out in the car."

Once they'd left, Cooper finally looked at me and said, "Yeah, so?"

"So?" I said. "So, is she, like, your girlfriend now or something?" I felt panicked—I wasn't in control of anything anymore, and I couldn't count on anyone.

"I don't know. Maybe," Cooper said, his eyes back on his feet.

"Maybe? But . . . *why*?"

"I don't know. Because I like her," he said. "She's cool. Look, it's no big deal. It's just a baseball game."

"Since when does she like baseball? And it *is* a big deal. This is only the single worst day of my life." Feeling a bit desperate, I said, "Look. I need you now, okay?" I instantly felt stupid for saying such an overly dramatic thing—even if it was true.

"I'm sorry, Loosh. Really. But I have plans." It might have been okay if he'd ended it with that; instead he added, "Not everything I do has to involve you, you know."

I felt like he had sucker punched me. "Fine," I managed. "Have fun on your date."

I ran all the way home, slamming our front door before the Nixons' car passed our house on its way to get Melanie.

★★★★★ 19 ★★★★★

I woke very early the next morning. It was still dark out. My bedside clock showed it was just after five o'clock. I'd had a horrible night, waking every so often feeling angry and anxious. I got out of bed, splashed water on my face, and tiptoed past Dad, asleep on the couch, and out the front door.

The air was brisk, and our street was eerily quiet. I hitched my bag up on my shoulder and walked quickly. I was wide awake.

I walked around to the side of the Nixons' house. Stepping carefully through a prickly bush, I crouched low and tapped on Cooper's window. There was no movement inside, so I tapped louder. Finally I heard him stumbling out of bed, and the blinds zipped up.

Cooper looked at me through half-open eyes for a moment—he probably thought he was still asleep.

"Wake up!" I said in a loud whisper.

He opened the window. "What time is it?"

"Come on," I said, stepping back from the window and through the bush. "Meet me at the garage."

Waiting outside the closed garage door, I didn't even notice the cold, even though my breath steamed out in front of my face. I concentrated on wrapping my hands, putting extra layers across the knuckles. Finally, the door rolled open, creaking along the way. Cooper switched on the light, then squinted against the brightness.

"It's Saturday," he mumbled.

"Get your gear on," I said, stepping inside.

"My hands." He held out his wraps.

"You really need to learn to do this yourself. Pay attention this time." As I wrapped Cooper's hands, I could still faintly smell last night's cologne, which made me wrap them a bit tighter than necessary.

"What's this about?" he asked.

"Blech," I said. "Dragon breath."

"Sorry," he muttered, turning his face.

"There," I said, finishing. "Come on, get your head-gear on."

"Okay, okay."

I went to the automated timer and turned it on. His

feet seemed to robotically take him to the other side of the garage to his corner. I could tell he was still very groggy, and when the buzzer sounded, I went at him fast and hard. It took two hits to wake him up properly.

"Dang, Lucia!" he said angrily, as he ducked behind his gloves. I threw a jab to his cheek, but he blocked it. "What happened to not in the face?"

"New rules," I said as I hit him with a one-two, landing a jab on his left shoulder.

"Fine then," he said. He stepped away, his gloves still by his face, but he wasn't backing down. We kept our eyes on each other intensely, like we never had before, and circled the ring, hands up, each waiting to make the next strike. I shuffled in close to him, and threw my whole body into an uppercut, which he blocked. The buzzer went off. We eyed each other as we went to our corners.

"You sure you want these new rules?" he panted. Never taking my eyes off him, I nodded. "Fine then. You asked for it."

When the buzzer went off again, we went at each other with equal speed. But before I could get my first punch out, Cooper popped me with a jab on my collarbone, making me stumble back a few paces. If I'd ever doubted that he'd been holding back his full strength, I didn't now. In fact, I wasn't even sure that *this* was his full strength.

I went back at him swinging—he blocked most of my punches, and the more frustrated I got, the more wildly I swung. I kept my focus on his dark brown eyes and those stupid freckles, and I swung harder, barely noticing where the punches landed. Cooper came back and stunned me again in the chest, temporarily knocking the wind out of me.

When I caught my breath, I looked back at him, and all at once I saw Melanie, the vending machines, and even Ms. Jenkins. I blocked a punch that came dangerously close to my face. I wound up and threw a hard uppercut, clenching my fist tight and twisting my wrist at the last possible moment. It was the best punch I had ever thrown, and it landed right between his legs.

At first he didn't make a sound—he just doubled over, the veins in his neck bulging, his gloved hands covering himself. He fell to his knees, then let out a howl that I was sure would wake up the whole neighborhood. I stood over him, panting, knowing I should apologize.

Cooper rested one gloved hand on the cement floor of the garage and took deep breaths. "You okay?" I asked through hard breathing. He panted, trying to suck in air through labored breaths. I thought of Henry's breathing exercises.

Cooper slowly pushed himself up off the floor. He stood up straight and, with utter calmness, looked me dead in the eyes and said, "Go home."

I tried to laugh it off. "Come on, Coop. Don't be a wimp. It was an accident."

He tore his gloves off with his teeth, then threw them to the ground. "It wasn't and you know it." As he took off his headgear, he said, "I really am sorry about the presidency. I'm sorry I wasn't at your beck and call last night. But I have a life, you know. And I'm tired of being your punching bag."

"My punching bag? Oh, that's real original. Did Melanie tell you to say that? You know, Cooper, she may like you now but give it two weeks, she'll be over you, just like she gets over everything else. You can't hold her attention."

I knew I'd gone too far. Cooper looked stunned for a moment, then he turned around, flipped off the light, and pushed the button to close the garage door. When he slammed the door behind him, I heard him lock it. I had to duck to get out before the garage doors closed me in, and when they connected with the driveway, the neighborhood was once again quiet. The sky had brightened slightly, but it was a gray morning, and the air felt heavy, like rain.

BLUE JAYS . . .
THE VIEW FROM ABOVE

Life Without Latham

BY NICOLE JEFFRIES

It's week two of Melanie O'Hare's reign as Angus's student council president and welcome changes are already being felt.

Her first order of business was to fix the disastrous mistake made by disgraced president Lucia Latham, those unpopular vending machines. The machines have now been completely restocked with new items, including organic but delicious popcorn, granola bars, and even low-fat candy. Said Ms. O'Hare, "It was totally clear that everyone wanted a change in them. I mean, all you had to do was read the signs." Ms.

O'Hare was referring to the vandalism often found on Ms. Latham's machines.

And, unlike her predecessor, Ms. O'Hare was quick to give credit where credit was due. "The whole idea was Cooper's," she said of Cooper Nixon, the council's secretary. "Once he suggested changing out the foods, we were all like, Duh. I can't believe we didn't think of it sooner."

The best part of this change is that the food is actually good—the very quality missing from Ms. Latham's idea of healthy fare. Furthermore, the items are selling.

"The spicy pita chips are so good," said seventh grader Cara Weaver, through a mouthful of that very food. "I could eat them every day."

Indeed, the items are selling. And this time around, the entire student council is getting into the act of promoting these wonderful new products. Says treasurer Jared Hensley, "We're doing a drawing to drive even more people to the machines to help make up for lost revenue," he explained. "Like, a local movie theater will donate tickets, then we'll secretly mark one of the machine's items. Whoever gets that food, wins!"

So, what's up next for this new student council? As announced by Ms. Jenkins, they'll be raising money for the football team, which needs new warm-up suits due to the unseasonably cold weather and unusually large number of players this year. And how will this new regime raise the funds?

"It's a bit of a surprise," teases Ms. O'Hare, looking striking in an emerald green knitted beret. "Let's just say I'm putting a whole new twist on the term 'bake sale.'"

More food choices from the new council? Somehow we think there's not a bad apple in this whole bunch.

★★★★★ 20 ★★★★★

I went through the days like a robot, not wanting to face anyone, talk to anyone, or deal with anyone. It was all a hazy memory, like a dream you only remember bits and pieces of.

Cooper had stopped me in the halls after I low-blowed him. He hadn't called me and I hadn't called him. As I walked toward third-period U.S. history, I passed him at his locker. I could barely look at him, much less talk to him, and once I walked by, he yelled, for everyone to hear, "All you have to do is say you're sorry!"

Cooper would always forgive me, I knew that much. But even though I really was sorry for hitting him, I was still having a hard time forgiving him. Why didn't he think I was cool? Did he know how it made me feel when he said that about Melanie? By not telling me, I felt like he was lying to me. And why, I wondered more and more, usually late at night before I fell asleep, didn't he think I was worthy of putting cologne on for, or tucking in his shirt and wearing a belt for?

I couldn't bring myself to face him. Not yet. And after reading in the school paper about all the brilliant ideas the new council was having (and stealing—like Jared ever had an original idea of his own), I was at a brand-new, all-time low. Why hadn't Cooper thought up the food-exchange idea when I was in office? I guess I wasn't an inspiring leader.

I'd tried to tell Mom about what happened. I thought she'd be logical, tell me that mistakes happen but that it's how you recover from them that really matters. But I didn't get a pep speech from her like I hoped.

"What do you want me to say, Lucia?" she asked one Sunday afternoon as she clipped coupons from the paper. "You made a huge error in judgment. Now you have to accept the consequences."

She looked at me with eyebrows raised, and I said, "How about, 'Everything will be okay?' How about, 'You're not a bad person and this will all blow over?' How can you be so harsh?"

She sighed and put down her scissors. "I'm sorry, honey. I know you're going through a rough time, but we all are." She tried to smile when she said, "We're all in this together."

Oh, please, I thought as I went back to my room to sulk. My mother speaking in clichés was a whole new low.

I even sought spiritual guidance from Henry. After I told him what went down, he said, "The ugly fish in the beautiful river is part of what makes the river beautiful."

"What?"

"You should treasure this ugly fish in your life's river," he continued, with a straight face. "Treasure it as much as all the beautiful fish. They're all a part of our journey downstream."

After that, I realized that the only person left to turn to was my dad.

It was Friday night, just after Nicole's article on how smashingly well the new student council was doing without me appeared. I wondered what I ever did to Nicole for her to write such negative stuff about me—she really seemed to have it in for me. And where was Mrs. Troxel through all this? Wasn't she supposed to approve everything before it was printed? Where were the checks and balances, the fair and unbiased reporting?

I made myself a sandwich and settled in front of the TV for reruns of my favorite crime show.

As I pried the sticky bread off the roof of my mouth, Dad came in and sat at the opposite end of the couch with a bag of barbeque chips and a bottle of name-brand beer. I wondered bitterly why he got fancy beer but I wasn't allowed my organic milk.

He let out a deep sigh and stared blankly at the TV. Mom was working late and Henry had just left for his friend Simon's house, where they were testing recipes. In addition to giving up all meat and fish, he'd recently given up root vegetables like carrots and potatoes, saying killing is killing since the plant dies when you uproot it. Mom told him if he wanted to be fed, he'd have to come up with simple alternatives she or Dad could fix at mealtimes.

"Henry's finally cracked," I told Dad through a mouthful of sticky bread.

"What now?" He took a gulp from his bottle, then set it on the coffee table in front of him.

"He's talking about ugly fish and beautiful rivers. He's totally not making sense."

"That's better than what Mom is saying," Dad said.

"She basically said I should get off my butt and go fishin' for a job."

I didn't say anything because what I wanted to say to him wasn't very nice. I didn't want to be mean or snarky to Dad—in spite of myself, I just wanted someone to talk to.

"I don't know what I'm supposed to do now," I said, both of us keeping our eyes on the television. A cop was interrogating a suspect, who was pretending he wasn't intimidated. "The student council was *my* thing. Now I don't have a . . . thing anymore."

Dad stuck his hand in the chip bag and said, "Don't I know what you mean."

"I mean, I've always been president. If anyone ever asked, 'Who is Lucia Latham?' all you had to do is look in the old yearbooks. You'd see it right there. 'Oh, she's the student council president. That's who she is.' But now I'm nothing. Just a regular student. Worse, actually. I'm a regular student who used to be somebody."

"I know the feeling." Dad sighed.

As the suspect on TV finally cracked and threw himself at the false mirror, I said, "You know what? I'm getting what I deserve. I always thought things could be so great, that I could do such amazing things as long as I tried hard enough. But from now on . . . forget it."

"Forget it," Dad repeated, his eyes on the TV, same as mine.

"I'm not saying I'm not going to try. I'm just going to keep my expectations low. That way, no matter how badly I bomb out, I won't be as disappointed. And I won't expect anything of anyone else, either." I nodded to myself, realizing that this was the way to live. The higher the expectations, the harder the fall. Everyone knew that.

"Well," I said to Dad, who took another swig of beer, his glassy eyes on the television, "I'm going to bed. Thanks for listening."

★★★★★ 21 ★★★★★

Before my resignation, in the days when I cared, I would wake up each morning with a solid plan of action for the day. Not anymore. With my new mantra of keeping my expectations low, I woke up with nothing to do—and nothing to worry about.

I thought this would make me feel better, but I realized that not thinking about anything made me think about a lot of things I didn't want to—like Cooper, who still wasn't talking to me because I still hadn't apologized to him, and also Melanie, whom I had to face on the school bus.

The one thing I had to acknowledge was the fact that Melanie had run for v.p. at my request. She didn't even want it. She barely paid attention in council meetings, and she showed no initiative in any projects. Now she was president.

It angered me that something I had taken such pride in and took so seriously was handed over to her even though she hadn't asked for it. She'd probably look at it as another fun project that wouldn't hold her interest through football season. And with the yearly fund-raiser coming up at the end of the week, she had to focus and actually raise all that money. The school, the students, the entire football team, and all their parents were expecting new warm-up suits, and she had to deliver. For once, Melanie had people depending on her and frankly, I wasn't sure she'd pull through.

The Monday after I had my talk with Dad—or, as I realized later, after I'd talked *to* Dad—I waited for the school bus on the corner as usual. And as had happened every day since the beginning of the school year, Melanie came running out of her house at the last minute, with whatever hat she was wearing that day threatening to fly off her head. But instead of waiting at the bus's door for her to arrive, for over a week now I quickly climbed the stairs, sat in the second seat on the right, and buried my face in a book. She always passed by me and sat a few rows back and usually started in on some unfinished homework (I could see this in the bus driver's mirror). We didn't say a word to each other, and we didn't even look at each other. But on this Monday, she decided to break our unspoken agreement.

She sat down heavily right next to me as the bus rumbled down the street. My heart raced. I didn't know how to feel toward her—I really didn't. I wanted to be mad at her for taking the two things that meant the most to me, but in my heart I knew she hadn't done anything wrong. I mean, she could have told me about Cooper, but other than that . . .

"Lucia," she said. "You have to talk to me sooner or later."

Henry had recently told me that being angry with someone is so unhealthy that it can actually break down your immune system and make you ill. I couldn't afford to come down with the flu, but being next to Melanie and her carefree attitude—and that hat, a tan fedora this time, always a new hat, how much money did she, did her *father*, spend on those things?!—made it hard for me to act like everything was fine.

"What should I talk to you about?" I asked, scooting closer to the window.

"Well, I don't know. The fact that you won't talk to me? You're not actually this mad at me, are you?"

She didn't sound like her usual peppy self. In fact,

she sounded a little whiny. That was weird because I didn't know what she had to complain about. After all, she had everything.

"I don't know," I said. "Should I be?"

"No," she said. "You shouldn't. I didn't do anything wrong, Lucia."

"Really?" I said, my face flushing hot, all of Henry's advice going right out the window. "Well then, I guess I'll just go ahead and say, *you're welcome*." She scrunched her eyes below the rim on her hat. "You're welcome for introducing you to my best friend. So glad the two of you have hooked up." Melanie clenched her jaw but said nothing. "And you're welcome for making you president of student council. Sounds like you're doing a fan-freaking-tastic job of it."

"Look." She scooted away to face me better. "I know it's impossible for you to admit, but I actually *am* doing a good job of it."

"So I read. Sounds like everyone is totally in love with you. You're like our generation's JFK."

"Why can't you give me any credit? I've never said anything bad about you. All I've done is try to come up with creative ideas, like for the fund-raiser. I think it'll take it to a whole new level than it's ever been in the past."

My hands clenched the bar of my backpack. "The bake sale is a *tried and true* way of doing things. It's *traditional*. And I could raise a ton of money. Just ask Cooper—he knows what a great job I always do."

"I'm confused," she said. "Is this about the presidency or Cooper?" I didn't answer, but stared defiantly out the window. "Look," she went on, "if you like Cooper, just say so. . . ."

"This has nothing to do with him," I said, but a bit too loudly. My face was totally red, I could feel it. "But I don't *like* him like him."

"Fine, sorry I asked," she muttered.

We finally pulled up to the school. "You know what? Just forget it." I pushed past her to get out of the seat, which was hard with my big backpack. I couldn't believe she thought I liked Cooper.

As I pounded down the steps of the bus, dragging my backpack behind me, one thought kept swirling in my confused head: *I do not like him.*

22

I was so mad I couldn't see straight. And, okay, I know I was being totally mean and irrational about Melanie but I couldn't help it. My feet simply stormed ahead of me down the halls, the wheels of my backpack squeaking angrily behind me.

I didn't know what her brilliant fund-raiser idea was, and maybe it was something good, but that didn't mean that after all my years as president and all the projects I'd worked on, she was better than me. And that's what I felt like she was saying.

And her suggesting I liked Cooper! Please. Please, please, please! He was like a brother to me. I didn't like him like *that,* and in fact, I didn't like him much at all right then, even though I sort of missed him and knew I had to apologize. But come on, the thought of kissing Cooper or even just holding his hand made me feel . . .

I was so lost in my thoughts that I wasn't even watching where I was going, and I rammed right into the boy himself. As I backed away from Coop, I looked into his eyes, then quickly looked away, reminding myself to breathe.

"Oh, s-sorry," I stammered.

He had his hand on my elbow, then seemed to realize he was touching me and quickly pulled it back. "You okay?" he asked, and I understood that he meant from our colliding, not from anything else.

"Yeah, I'm fine," I said. I could barely face him after what Melanie had suggested, but I felt like I was stuck to the spot. I hardly noticed the students pushing past us and wondered, a bit confused, why I had never noticed the bump on the bridge of his nose before.

Oh, God. Why was I thinking like that? *It's Cooper,* I told myself. *Cooper!*

"So . . . ," he began.

"So."

"I'm glad I ran into you," he said.

"Really?"

"Yeah. Well, I don't mean literally run into you. I'm glad we're seeing each other." I looked down at my brown loafers, feeling so happy that he still wanted to talk to me and that he didn't hate me.

"Listen, Coop." I reminded myself not to get my hopes up. After what I did to him and what I'd said, I deserved to be friendless. So, with my expectations appropriately low, I said, "I'm really sorry. About everything, but especially, uh, about hitting you. I was just upset about the whole impeachment thing and I guess, I mean, I *know* I took it out on you. I didn't mean to make you my punching bag." I made myself look into his eyes when I said, "You're my best friend." They were the same words he'd said to me just a few weeks ago, and I realized that saying them out loud meant everything.

"It's okay. This might sound dumb, but I sort of missed you. Like with boxing and stuff. Anyway," he said, "I have to talk to you about something, and you're the only person who will understand."

I said something like, "Mmm-hmm." Honestly, I couldn't focus, and I couldn't understand what I was feeling. I kept telling myself, *This is just Cooper!* But when did his lips get so red and fluffy?

"Don't tell anyone I told you, but Melanie is on the verge of blowing this fund-raiser." I stared back at him blankly. "She has this crazy idea, and the whole thing is going to be a huge failure."

"You want me to help Melanie."

He nodded sheepishly. "Loosh, you don't understand what she has planned. It's going to explode in her face. Possibly literally. I heard Jared talking about it in the halls with his friends. Can't you just offer to help?"

"Melanie and I aren't talking. In fact, I'm pretty sure we're not even friends anymore."

"Why?" he asked. I looked at him severely, like *How could you not know?!* "Come on, don't be like that. You apologized to me, you can apologize to her."

"Who says I'm the one who should be doing all the apologizing?"

"Well, what'd we do?"

Cooper Nixon just called himself and Melanie O'Hare a "we."

He didn't understand what she had taken from me, whether it was on purpose or not. He didn't know that she might be a better president than I was and that I'd been wasting my time all these years. He didn't care how I was doing now that everything I cared about had been snatched away from me. I was sad. I was tired. Cooper looked at me with big, brown eyes and fluffy red lips, and without realizing what I was doing, I leaned in and kissed him. Right on the mouth.

It was my first kiss, and I felt it immediately. It lasted only a moment, but everything around us seemed to fade away, and I felt all melty. When I pulled back, my heart seemed to fold in on itself, and I even felt a little faint, which I think is technically called "swooning." I slowly opened my eyes, and that's when I saw Cooper's wide-open eyes staring at me in a way that can only be described as shocked. And not in the pleasantly surprised kind of way, either.

"Oh my God," I said, touching my hand to my lips.

"Why did you do that?" he said. Actually, more like demanded.

"I—I don't know," I said honestly. *He didn't like it. He's totally grossed out. He hates me even more now.* "I'm sorry."

Cooper looked around us, and I realized, with absolute relief, that there was no one in the halls. But now I was going to be late for class.

"I—I gotta get to class," Cooper said without looking at me, then quickly turned and walked away. As I stood alone in the halls, still touching my mouth, I wondered if my life could get any worse. Kissing Cooper actually felt good. I would have thought it would be like kissing my brother, but it wasn't. It was like kissing a boy. And I liked it.

But he hadn't.

I wanted to take it back. I wanted to take everything back. This was supposed to be my best year of junior high and to prepare me for high school, but I'd only made things go horribly wrong. But with this, with Cooper, I *had* to fix it. I refused to go any longer without my best friend. Because that's what was important—Cooper, as my best friend. I would never admit it out loud, but I was glad my first kiss ever was with Cooper Nixon, even if it was our last kiss ever.

Later that same day (was it actually still only Monday?!), I rushed toward the cafeteria to find Cooper. I got there just before he went inside, and I grabbed his wrist and pulled him to the side of the vending machine before he even knew what was happening. When he got a good look at me, he said, "Uh, Lucia, seriously. I really like you as a friend, but . . ."

"Oh, stop it. I'm not going to kiss you again."

He looked at me skeptically. "You're not?" I shook my head. I saw his face start to relax, the old Coop looking back at me. "Promise?"

"I swear, I promise I will never in my life ever try to kiss you again."

He cracked a smile and said, "Thank God."

I covered my face with my hands, mortified at the whole thing. "Oh my God, I am so sorry. Please, can we just forget that ever happened?"

"Not sure if that's possible," he said. "But it's cool. I always knew you were in love with me." For the second time that day, the world stopped and so did my breathing. Maybe he did . . . "Kidding, Loosh. Dang, take a breath or something, you look like you're about to pass out."

"I'm such a mess."

"Clearly." He laughed.

We stood for a moment as the last of our grade filed into the cafeteria. I told myself that later I would reprogram my mind to think about Cooper the way I used to—as a friend and not a guy. I figured with enough self-discipline, I could brainwash myself.

"I can't believe all the drama I've created," I said, eager to change the subject. "Does everyone still hate me for fudging the vote?"

"Nah," Cooper said. "I don't even think they remember anymore. Now everyone's talking about the new cheerleading coach. Did you see Nicole's article on it?"

I had. Apparently, April DeHart's dad had paid for an outside cheer coach, which was against district rules. I could take a hit with Nicole's stories, but I wasn't sure April could.

"I think Nicole is getting more ruthless," I said. "She was there in the meeting when I had the idea of a contest to boost vending-machine sales, and then her article made it sound like it was Jared's idea."

"I know. I kind of schooled her on that."

"You did?" He shrugged, like it was no big deal. "What'd you say?"

"I don't remember. I was just mad about the article in general. She made it sound like we were all so happy without you."

Which was exactly what I had been wondering. "But aren't you? I mean, you didn't come to me after you read it."

He put his hands in his baggy jeans pockets and looked out the side door. "I know. I really was mad at you. Not just for the hit but for, like . . ." He paused. "Sometimes it was like I wasn't allowed to have any friends but you. You've gotten sort of . . . *bossy* over the last couple of years."

I felt myself cringe. I had been motivated to be taken

seriously and to leave my mark on the school. But I didn't know I'd been bossy. I really didn't. "Why didn't you tell me?"

"I don't know. Whatever, I'm telling you now. I didn't *not* like you, so stop looking like you're going to vomit or something." He lightly punched my shoulder. "Just lighten up or something. You don't have to be so serious all the time."

"Oh, don't worry. I'm definitely on a new mission."

He smiled. "Listen. I was serious about what I said before about Melanie and the fund-raiser. Will you say something to her? Maybe just subtly offer to help her or something?"

"I don't think she'll want my help," I said. "I told you, we're not talking. We got into a huge fight this morning on the bus."

"Really?"

I nodded but didn't elaborate. He seemed to understand and didn't ask any questions.

"I know you don't want anything to mess up the fund-raiser," he continued. "Raising the money is what's important, right? Just say something to her. Don't tell her I said this, but she might ruin it all."

I sighed. I didn't want that either. "Fine. I will only

because you want me to. And I'm telling you, she's not going to like it."

"Just try," he pressed.

If I was truly keeping my expectations low, then I shouldn't expect her to welcome my assistance with open arms. Before even saying a word to Melanie, I knew she'd hate my butting in.

"Come on," he said, tugging on my hand. *Zing!* I thought of how jealous I'd been when he grabbed Melanie's wrist on the trampoline. "Let's do it now, get it over with."

"No way! I'll do it, but not now. After lunch." I certainly didn't want an audience for this.

"Fine," he said.

"And for the record," I said as we headed toward the cafeteria, away from where Melanie sat with Rose Andreas and Catherine Collins, "I'm only doing this for you and the football team. Not her."

I was thankful that Cooper sat with me, even though he kept looking toward Melanie like he'd rather be sitting with her.

When the bell rang, I told Cooper I'd see him later as I headed toward Melanie and her friends.

"Good luck," he cheered. "And thanks!"

"Hey," I said as I approached Melanie, trying to sound casual, but my heart was pounding and I could feel Rose's and Catherine's eyes on me. After this, I would be totally paid up on my debt to Cooper. "Um, can I talk to you for a sec?" She told her friends she'd see them later, then turned to face me.

"Look," she said before I even began. "About this morning. I'm really sorry."

"You don't have to apologize. I was the bigger jerk. I'm just all messed up because of the whole . . . thing."

"I know," she said. "It's okay."

"Look, I know you have something really big planned for the fund-raiser. I just wanted to say, if you need any help on it or anything, just let me know."

"Really?" She sounded like she didn't believe me.

"Yes."

"Well, thanks for offering," she said, "but I'm pretty sure I've got it covered."

"Yeah, well. I just thought I'd offer. I have a lot of experience with fund-raisers."

Melanie looked off down the hall, where Cooper was standing by a water fountain as if he were trying to decide whether he was thirsty. "You don't think I can do it, do you?" I hated to admit it, but truthfully I didn't think she could, given her track record and the fact that Cooper had asked me to help save the whole thing. But by thinking all this just after she asked me, I guess my silence gave her the answer. "I can do this," Melanie said defiantly, "without you. You'll see."

"Melanie, that's not what—"

But she was already running down the hall, right past Cooper without stopping. I turned and headed in the other direction.

"Loosh, wait up!"

When Cooper caught up to me, I said, "I can't believe I just did that." I'd never had faith that Melanie could follow through with anything, but I didn't know that she knew I thought that. It made me feel horrible for thinking it in the first place.

"What happened?"

"Forget it," I told him. "She can do it on her own."

"Come on, Loosh. You have to help her."

I stopped and faced Cooper, even though I was so totally going to be late for class. "No, Cooper. She has to do it on her own. Don't you get it?"

"No, I don't!"

I started walking again. "She'll do fine. I'm sure the whole thing is going to be great." I said the words, but I didn't believe them.

"Stop being like that!" he said, but I wasn't *being like that.* I was trying to be a good friend to Melanie by giving her space to make her own mark. Was that so awful?

"Loosh, would you please stop?" Cooper begged, trying to keep pace with me.

I kept walking until Cooper finally backed off. It wasn't until I got to my locker that I realized he'd never told me what she planned to do.

23

The annual fund-raiser began on Friday during seventh period and went into the after-school hours. Parents left work early to stop by and check it all out, and of course almost everyone loved getting out of class an hour early. That day I didn't mind missing class—I was as anxious as everyone else to see what Melanie had planned, even though I still had a hard time believing I wouldn't be a part of it.

As Nicole had written in my resignation story, this year the goal was to raise money for new, and extra, warm-up suits for the football team. The weather was still unseasonably cold, the team had more players than usual, and there were districtwide budget cuts on athletics programs in general, all adding up to our guys' needing some extra sweat suits. The plaque announcing which class donated the suits would go in the guys' locker room. With Melanie's name as president. I tried to console myself by telling myself that having my name in the guys' locker room would have been a little tacky, but I didn't really buy it.

When the bell rang ending sixth period and the day, I headed toward the cafeteria with the other excited students with a mixture of enthusiasm, dread, and loneliness. In the past two years, the eighth-grade president had always asked for my help since I was so reliable. I tried to embrace the lightness of having no responsibility and just enjoy the event, but I was worried about Melanie. I didn't want her to fail, but I was also nervous that she'd be better than me on her first try.

The cafeteria was utterly transformed. Thick sheets of clear plastic covered most of the floor, and the lunch tables were folded and lined up against the walls. Banners and balloons, in our school colors of light blue and orange, decorated the ceiling and walls, and someone had drawn a cartoon of a shivering football player and hung it in the center of the back wall.

When I saw the pies that were stacked haphazardly on two long tables, I got that bad feeling in my stomach. Some were already out of their boxes and none looked particularly appetizing. But then I saw what was in front of the table of pies—the two wooden cutouts with holes to put your own face in—and I realized that this wasn't a bake sale. The pies were there to be thrown, at people, with their heads stuck through those horrible wooden cutouts.

The first was a man in a suit, holding a briefcase in one hand and waving with the other, waiting for someone to give him a face. The second was a blond woman in a pink bikini with her hand on her hip, which was popped out at a sexy angle. A sign next to them read, Pie Your Favorite Teacher—$5 for 3 Throws!

Students clamored in front of the table to pay for a shot at the teachers. Coach Fleck stood before the cutouts talking to a couple of the female teachers—among them Mrs. Peoria, whose arms were folded tightly across her body and whose face was wearing a clearly angry look.

"Come on, folks," cheered Jared, who clutched a handful of bills in his hand like a street cards dealer I'd seen on cop shows. "This is your chance to get back at your favorite teachers for that pop quiz! Come on, Michael," he called to the team's quarterback, Michael Rutter. "Cream Coach Fleck for all those suicides he makes y'all run!"

Someone bumped me from behind, eager to get to the front and pay their money. I saw Cooper bringing out more pies from the kitchen and went over to him.

"You came!" he said as he stacked pies in a precarious tower. "I might be wrong about this whole thing. Jared already has a fistful of money."

I didn't want to be the know-it-all, but I couldn't help but feel extremely cautious. I tried to sound light as I said, "Did Melanie buy all these pies?"

"Yeah." I made a face, and Cooper said, "I know, I know. That's what I was worried about. But Melanie kept saying it's an investment, and I'm starting to think that maybe she's right. We've made a ton of money already." He looked out at the scene and said, "Anyway, it's too late now."

Mrs. Weeks walked into the cafeteria, and I watched as her jaw went limp at the sight of the bikini cutout. "Have the teachers agreed to do this?" I asked.

"Coach Fleck is in. He was the one who helped Melanie find the cutouts. He's still trying to rally more teachers. He was supposed to do it sooner, but Melanie only asked him this morning, so . . ."

A huddle of women English and math teachers stood off to the side, talking quickly, with hard looks on their faces. "Uh, do you think the female teachers are going to be offended by the bikini cutout?"

"Why?" he asked, licking whipped cream off his fingers.

"Cooper," I began, pointing to the cutouts, "you've got a guy wearing a suit but the woman is wearing a bikini. That's totally sexist."

"No!" Cooper bristled. "It's funny! I bet we can get Coach Fleck behind the bikini one, too. He's down for anything. Look," he said. "I have to get back there." He nodded toward the kitchen. "Make sure you buy a throw, okay? We might need the money."

I looked around at the tables filled with pies and hoped that I was wrong about the whole thing.

"Attention, Blue Jays!" called Melanie over a microphone that someone had handed her. "I'd like to welcome everyone to our first annual Pie Throw!" Some kids clapped and whooped. "I want to remind everyone that the pies you throw will be for a good cause. Our fighting Blue Jays are still on a winning streak but freezing their buns off during this cold weather! So hand over that money, pick up a pie, and cream your favorite teacher!"

A few kids clamored in front of Melanie to buy a pie,

but so far, it looked like only Coach Fleck had volunteered to be a target. I watched Melanie work the crowd so easily, making students laugh and goading them into buying double the amount of pies they had intended. She wore a chocolate-colored derby and her eyes were bright with the thrill of having accomplished something wonderful. I wondered, for the first time, why she wore hats every day. Were they some sort of security blanket for her, like hiding behind glasses or extremely long hair?

Cooper came out of the kitchen with more pies, and when he saw Melanie working the crowd, a smile spread across his face, and I felt a pang in the pit of my stomach.

"And now," Melanie announced after Jared had collected even more money, "it's time for Coach Fleck to assume the position!"

Coach Fleck put his head through the wooden hole of the man in the suit. Quarterback Michael Rutter missed Coach Fleck with his first throw. "I expect more from you, Rutter!" Coach Fleck taunted. The guys around Michael laughed and shoved him, and Michael looked more serious when he pulled back his pie arm and chucked the next pie with more force. This time, it landed square on Coach Fleck's face. He looked stunned, but then licked the cream off the sides of his mouth and laughed. "Pretty good!"

Another football player shoved Michael aside for his shot at Coach Fleck, and although he grazed Coach with the first hit, his other two splattered on the board beside him.

As more guys hit Coach Fleck, each seemed to hit him harder and harder. From where I stood it looked like it hurt, but Coach Fleck never let on. He decided to take a break (the football players booed him) and then something inexplicable happened. Mrs. Miller, a stocky woman who taught economics and wore out-dated glasses, got behind the faceless bikini woman. All the guys started whooping wildly, running up to the tables to hand over their money. I had a bad feeling in my stomach, but when I looked at Melanie, she wore the same ecstatic expression beneath her brown derby. Wade Lazcano stepped up, and he threw his pie at Mrs. Miller with such force you'd think he was pitching for the Rangers. The pie didn't just hit Mrs. Miller right in the face, but it knocked her glasses off, landing them on the floor in a puddle of cream.

Mrs. Miller tried to laugh, but she pulled her head

out of the hole and said to the jeering crowd, "I think that's all this old woman can handle!" I felt horrible for her as she came around to the front of the bikini woman to pick up her glasses, but I gasped as she bent down and Wade nailed her in the butt with another pie.

The crowd cried, *"Oooo!"* Melanie playfully reprimanded Wade, but she was laughing, too. Then Ms. Jenkins came over and warned Melanie in a stern voice that I could barely hear over the crowd, "Melanie, keep this under control!"

"Yes, ma'am," she said while wiping tears of laughter from her eyes. "Y'all, seriously!" she called to the crowd. "Be nice!"

With everyone crowding around the pie table to get a better view of the smashing, Shawn Foster shoved Donnie Schaffer into the pies, and Donnie landed with his arm covered in cream. Shawn laughed, but Donnie picked up the ruined pie and held it threateningly at Shawn.

"Dude, don't even." Shawn laughed. They were barely arm's length apart, but Donnie pulled back his arm and smashed the pie into his friend's face; that was all the crowd needed. After that, it was total pie pandemonium.

Pies flew everywhere. People just started grabbing them from the tables and hitting anyone who was close by. The teachers, who had been huddled against the wall, scrambled out the door, apparently feeling no need to step in and stop the chaos. Mrs. Weeks screamed, "Children! Please!" while Coach Fleck roughly grabbed the players he could reach by their arms. Their fellow teammates saved them by smacking pies right on top of Coach Fleck's head. Ms. Jenkins stomped toward Melanie in her sensible low heels but slipped on the creamy mess, landing with a thud. I ducked from pies that flew like bullets across the room and made my way over to her.

"Are you okay?" I called to Ms. Jenkins over the fray. Her face blazed with anger. I tried to help her up but her heels slipped and down she plopped again.

Coach Ryan came to help her up, and she made a pained expression as he did so. Melanie was screaming at the people around her to stop.

Ducking pies as I went, I grabbed Melanie's upper arm; she whirled around to face me. "What?" she demanded, her eyes wild, and I wondered if she had any measure of composure left in her.

"Melanie, get the microphone! You've got to make everyone stop!"

Her eyes finally seemed to see me, and they were filled with tears. I thought she was going to ask for my help, but instead she yelled, "I can do this by myself!" Someone behind her called her name, and when she turned around she was greeted with a pie right to her head, knocking her chocolate-brown derby to the cream-slicked floor. Melanie let out a horrid scream, as if a wig had been removed to reveal a bald head.

With splatters of pie all over me, I bent down to pick up her ruined hat. When I handed it to her, her hands were shaking. She pulled the hat down tight over her head. And as the cafeteria sunk further and further into chaos, Melanie briefly took in the scene, then shoved past me and ran out the doors.

BLUE JAYS . . .
THE VIEW FROM ABOVE

P-Day at Angus

BY NICOLE JEFFRIES

Who would have thought there'd be a day when we'd all wish Lucia Latham was still our president?

A fierce and unexpected battle raged during what should have been a joyous, generous fund-raiser last week. Friday was P-Day (Pie Day) at Angus, and our cafeteria, like the bloodied beaches of Normandy, became a bona fide battle-field. This time, though, pies were the weapon of choice, along with a heavy artillery of sexism, not to mention outright disregard for authority.

The first annual Pie Toss, brainchild of inexperienced president Melanie O'Hare, was supposed to be a chance for the eighth-grade student council to raise money in a unique and spirited way, and to leave their mark on their class for years to come. But instead of raising money for the football team's much-needed warm-up suits, this year's council made its mark by being the first-ever fund-raiser to actually lose money.

The ill-fated Pie Toss began omi-nously, with Coach Fleck taking a hard hit to the face by his own quarter-back, Michael Rutter. As if that and the bikini-clad female cutout weren't bad enough, things spiraled further out of control, finally erupting in absolute anarchy that not even Ms. Jenkins could control. Ms. O'Hare herself ran out of the cafeteria, leaving her mess behind for others to clean up. It wasn't until school custodian Mickey Shroud stretched a water hose from the kitchen and sprayed down the students that any order was restored.

Although Jared Hensley collected a stack of money prior to the outbreak, all money has been ordered back to the school to repay the extensive damages the cafeteria suffered, not to mention the cost of the pies purchased for throwing, which were bought at Ms. O'Hare's discretion at Sugar Pie's Bakery.

School damages include two ruined cash registers, two speakers, a microphone, the American flag, plus additional cleaning needed for the floor and windows.

Furthermore, two students were injured, both by slipping on the floor—cheerleader April DeHart sprained her wrist, and seventh grader Cory Atkinson cracked his elbow. Even our own principal, Ms. Jenkins, suffered a broken tailbone. Coach Ryan, never one to leave a soldier behind, quickly came to help Ms. Jenkins off to safety while dodging pies like so many German bullets on those beaches of Normandy.

We can only hope that Ms. O'Hare has learned the painful lesson that our own principal learned—that rushing into a situation before considering the outcome will lead to disastrous consequences.

★★★★★ 24 ★★★★★

"This is so good," I said to Cooper a week after the pie toss as we sat on his trampoline, huddled in blankets and sipping Mexican hot chocolates his mom had brought out. The school paper lay between us, and I nudged it away from me with my blanket-covered toe. I took another sip of the rich, chocolatey drink, feeling it slip through me, sending immediate comfort through my veins. I couldn't help but think that however Melanie was feeling at that exact moment, a sip of this would make her feel one iota better.

Cooper sat next to me on the trampoline, staring off toward the back of his house, not really listening. He'd been different since the pie toss—very quiet, almost pensive. Sad, I guess. I wondered what was going on between him and Melanie. Not that he ever talked about her around me, but there was something new in his silence that made me a little bit worried for him.

Melanie, on the other hand, had turned her massive failure into a big joke, laughing loudly with anyone who teased her about the pie debacle. Her locker had been decorated with pictures of pies cut out from magazines, and I couldn't help but wonder if she was the one who'd put them there.

As for how she acted toward me, she did nothing more than walk past me silently on the bus.

"Hey," I said to Cooper. "You there? How's Melanie *really* handling this whole thing?"

He turned his eyes down to the inside of his mug and shrugged. "I don't know. She blew up at me on Friday and hasn't really talked to me since."

"Why'd she blow up at you?"

"Said I let her take the fall alone."

"But she's president," I said. "And it was her idea." It was both the wonderful and the totally worst thing about being boss—good or bad, it all came down to you. Like, you could spar with the best and have the most amazing coach and cut-man and promoter and whatever else, but everything that goes on in that ring is all down to you.

"I didn't try to argue with her, and she hasn't talked to me since."

"I don't get it," I said, wondering how far I could tread without upsetting Cooper any more than he already was. "Because it seems like she's talking to everyone else about it. Every time I pass her she's joking about what a beautifully spectacular event it was. I heard her tell Shawn Keane that it was worth getting in trouble for."

Still staring into his mug, Cooper said, "I'm not even sure we're still together."

Cooper looked absolutely miserable. His shoulders were all slumped, and his eyes looked heavy and burdened. I wanted to at least put my hand on his knee, pat his back or something, but I didn't want to spook him again. Plus, I was still detoxing myself of those feelings I'd had of him. I expected to make a full recovery.

"Why do you say that?" I asked him.

"I don't know. Can you still be together when you haven't talked in a week?" Cooper's cheeks flushed pink, and I could tell he was getting riled up. "She won't answer when I call, she doesn't return my texts or e-mails, and she totally avoids me at school. I left her a note in her locker, you know, just telling her that the pie toss *was* a good idea, but I'm not even sure that's what she wants to hear, because you're right, she does joke all the time to everyone but me about what happened." Cooper let out a deep breath, then sipped his hot chocolate.

I wanted to tell him that it was really crappy of Melanie to be so mean to him. He'd never done anything but be nice to her. I understood that she was feeling low—who could understand better than me?—but I also learned, the hard way, that you can't take your anger out on innocent people. Which made me realize, with a pang to my heart, that Melanie and I had both misused Cooper's generosity. I had been no better to Cooper than Melanie was being to him now, and that made me feel ashamed.

When I looked out toward our street, I noticed a red dot bobbing down the sidewalk. I nudged Cooper. "Melanie," I said.

As he turned to look, there was a pained, hopeful look in his eyes. She turned up his driveway, and Cooper tossed the rest of his hot chocolate on the ground, then dropped the mug on the dead grass.

"Want me to leave?" I asked, but Cooper didn't say anything. When I scooted to the edge of the trampoline to get down, Melanie was close enough to say to me, "You don't have to go." I sat back, wondering what she would say. She was wearing her magic red hat, and I wondered why she needed it today.

She stood before the trampoline, looking between the springs for a moment. "I figured you'd both be here," she said, and I wondered if I heard an accusing tone in her voice. She looked up at Cooper, but quickly turned her attention back to the springs. "So anyway," she said quickly, "I guess that's it then." For a moment she didn't say anything more, and I wondered if she was talking about him or the student council. Melanie looked at me, her clear brown eyes boring straight into mine before she again turned back to the springs. "I'm done. I have about as much to do with the student council now as you do," she finally said.

My heart raced. "You can't quit. That's what everyone expects you to do."

She rolled her eyes, and I could tell she was only feigning indifference. "I wish. Mrs. Peoria actually thinks I did it just to get kicked off. Everyone knew I didn't want to be president. Mrs. P said she wasn't about to go through the trouble to replace me, but she did take away all my power." Melanie laughed at this. "Whatever, I don't care. She's right—I didn't want to be president. You know that."

I realized so many things at once. That Melanie used to always gloss over her problems with a smile and a joke, but twice now she had faced them—now, and when she'd approached me on the bus. And I didn't even recognize her bravery in doing this.

I also realized, fully and finally, that I had forced Melanie into a position she'd never wanted any part of, a position I knew she wasn't cut out for. My own need for power and success at any price not only led to my own downfall, but it also put Melanie in this position now. "Melanie," I began, "I'm really sorry about everything. I never should have asked you to—"

"It's fine, whatever," she interrupted. "It was fun for a couple of weeks, and what better way to go out than with P-Day? I mean, I couldn't have hoped for a better ending." Even as she spoke, I could tell she was lying, even if she didn't know it.

Finally, she looked at Cooper. So did I. My heart raced for him. He look petrified, like he couldn't speak even if he wanted to. She smiled at him, but it was a sad smile, and my stomach clenched at what was coming next. I wished I was anywhere but there. "Coop," she said. She tossed her hair off her shoulder, and I knew she was pretending like it was no big deal. "Look, I'm sorry but . . . you know." She plucked the springs with her fingernail. "Thanks for, um, being cool and everything."

Cooper sat with his eyes scrunched up, his mouth hanging slightly open.

"So anyway," Melanie said definitively. "I guess I'll see y'all around." She gave us each one last look, then turned around and walked off.

It wasn't until she'd turned back onto the road that Cooper seemed to find his voice. "What," he said, "was *that*?" He stood up on the trampoline and strained his neck to get a better view of her. "Did she just break up with me? Is that what that was?" I didn't know if he actually wanted me to respond, so I kept my mouth shut. Yeah, she hadn't handled it perfectly, but at least she had tried. Cooper looked down at me and asked, "Is it?"

I understood how angry he was. I thought of the morning I'd forced him to box me, then sucker punched him. "I don't know," I said.

"'I'm sorry, thanks for everything'? Is that how you break up?"

"Coop, sit down," I said, hoping it would calm him down. That's what people on TV and in movies always seemed to do. He dropped down on the trampoline, spilling my hot chocolate, now cold, on the blanket. I didn't say anything but tossed what was left on the grass and held the empty mug.

"You were right," Cooper said. "I should have listened to you. She totally bailed just like you said she would."

"No, Coop," I said. Maybe her bailing had something to do with her mom. Whatever it was, I didn't think she meant to be mean or cold. "I think she's just upset about everything."

"So she breaks up with me? Please. She doesn't care about anyone but herself. And she dumped me in front of you! Not that I care, but dang. You don't break up in front of other people, do you?" he asked, as if I knew anything about dating.

"No," I said, "you don't." I decided not to say anything more. Sometimes it felt good to be mad for a little while, and between Melanie and me, Cooper had definitely earned that right.

We sat on the trampoline until it was dark. I realized, as he alternately ranted and sulked, that I would never try to kiss him again. His friendship meant more to me than any romantic thing ever could. Besides, even if he felt the same way about me, we'd eventually break up—we were only thirteen, for crying out loud. What would we be like post–boyfriend/ girlfriend? We'd never again be like we were now. And the way we were now was the best way to be. Best friends. Always.

★★★★★ 25 ★★★★★

At home, I sat on my bed after I'd finished my homework, holding Paddy, and thought about everything that had happened.

I had expected my eighth-grade year to be my best, but instead it had turned into a muddled mess that I never could have predicted—and I wasn't even through the first semester yet. Then I realized, sitting alone in my quiet room, that despite all the change that had been happening in my life—at school, with my friends, in my life's ambition—that almost nothing had changed at home. That is, until we were called for dinner.

Dad made dinner. It'd been a long time since he'd cooked, and by the looks of things, Henry had convinced him to try some of his new vegetarian grub. Dad made falafel from a boxed mix; picked up hummus and pitas at the market; and cut up some tomatoes, cucumbers, onions, and lettuce.

"What's this?" Mom asked, looking skeptically at her plate.

"It's Mediterranean," Dad said. "You'll like it."

"And no animals were killed in the making of this meal," Henry added, nodding at Dad.

"You made this together?" I asked.

"Yep. Henry's idea." Dad smiled.

I had to admit I was a little jealous that Dad and Henry had worked together on something. Dad and I hadn't done anything in months. It seemed like the days of him taking me to his gym to work the bag were long gone.

"How are we supposed to do this?" Mom asked, peeking inside her pita as if the answer might be hidden there.

"Pack it in," Dad said. She looked at him like he had just suggested she smear the putty-colored hummus on her face. "Here," Dad said, getting up. "I'll do it. It's like a sandwich."

"It *is* a sandwich. It's Egyptian," Henry said, tucking falafel balls into his pita, then spooning the hummus on top of them and adding the vegetables. He topped that with another dollop of hummus. I mimicked him.

"What's that weird brown stuff?" Mom asked, but she seemed amused that Dad was making her pita for her. I noticed that he picked out the extra-thin-sliced tomatoes for her, just like she liked.

"Hummus. It's mashed chickpeas, mostly," Dad said. "There." He presented the plate back to Mom. "Do you know how to say 'bon appétit' in Egyptian, Henry?"

"Mmm, no," he said. "But let's hope this food nourishes our bodies as well as our minds."

I only wanted to gag a little bit, but I still smiled at my little brother.

Dad sat down and watched Mom as she picked up her pita, hesitated, then took a bite. She slowly began to nod. "Hmm!" she said through a mouthful. "It's good!"

Dad beamed, then chomped into his own. I was pretty sure that Mom hadn't complimented him in a long time, and was glad that she did tonight, in front of Henry and me.

"Speaking of food," I began in a pathetic attempt to get some attention focused on me. "Did anyone hear about the fund-raiser the school had last week?"

"Evelyn at work told me about it," Mom said. She looked at Dad and said, "Pie toss turned into a pie fight."

"Ah." Dad nodded, looking amused.

"It's worse than that," Henry said. "My friend Simon's sister said that almost a hundred pies were totally wasted for no good reason at all. Think of all those eggs in those pies, and all those chickens that had to lay those eggs in cramped quarters for *nothing*."

I sighed. For a guy who supposedly meditated every morning, Henry sure knew how to rile himself up. "That," I said, "and the student council lost money for the first time in its history. *Ever,*" I emphasized in case anyone missed it. I shook my head. "A travesty."

"How's Melanie taking it?" Mom asked, wiping the corner of her mouth.

"Not so well," I said, enjoying having someone to talk to about it. "I mean, she wants everyone to believe she's fine, but I'm not so sure. She's just laughing it off and making a joke of it. She wasn't kicked off the council, but it's like she's already quit."

"Really?" Dad asked, sounding surprised.

"Yes," I said, feeling uneasy with the way he was looking at me.

"Huh," was all he said.

Then Mom asked Henry what he was working on at school, and he launched into a speech about getting yoga included in PE, leaving me in silence to wonder why Dad kept darting his eyes at me when he thought I wasn't looking.

After dinner, Dad insisted he clean the kitchen even though Mom said it wasn't fair that he had to cook *and* clean (!). So, she kissed his cheek (double !) and went back to the bedroom with her laptop clutched to her chest. Henry told us all "peace" and went to his room, and I went to the living room, pulled a blanket over my lap, and turned on the TV to watch my favorite crime investigation show.

When Dad finished the dishes, he sat down in the chair next to the couch with a glass of ice water and let out a satisfied sigh.

We watched the show in silence for a good half hour, until a commercial came on for a heavyweight rematch on pay-per-view.

When it was over, Dad muttered, "Hmph." I looked at him, tired of wondering what he was thinking, and if he was getting at something.

"What?"

"Reminds me of something," he said. He shifted in his chair. "You remember watching fights with Naseem Hamed?"

"Prince Naseem?" I corrected. I couldn't believe he was bringing this fighter up—I had just been thinking about him a couple of weeks ago.

Dad smiled. "You know he's not a real prince. That was just a nickname he gave himself. Part of his arrogance."

"Of course," I said, even though I hadn't known. "What about him?"

"Didn't you ever wonder what happened to him?"

"He lost that big fight to Marco Antonio Barrera."

"Yeah. And?"

"And that was it," I said. "I guess his career ended."

Dad said, "In every big fight, there's always a clause that gives the fighters the option of a rematch. Hamed lost the fight, but he could have fought again. He just chose not to. And look what happened."

Dad sat back, like everything was obvious. "So?" Dad said.

"So, what?" I asked.

"Girl, aren't you ready for your rematch?" I looked at him blankly, and he said, "All that student council stuff. Like you talked about at dinner."

I tried not to sigh loudly. I thought I'd been pretty clear as to how things stood with me as far as student council was concerned. "There's no rematch. Against who? Melanie?" I shook my head. "The bout's over for me, Dad. I'm not even in the ring anymore. I'm not even in the *gym*."

"That's because you've chosen not to be. You can still fight, Lucia. You can still step back in."

I said, "I'm not going to try to get Mrs. Peoria or Ms. Jenkins to take me back as president. That'd be pathetic, and besides, Melanie is still president. Even if she doesn't want to be."

"Loosh, that's not what I'm talking about. You can still help things, can't you? You can help Melanie."

"Dad, she won't—"

"What was the first thing I taught you about boxing?" he asked.

"To keep yourself protected," I said automatically.

"No," he said. "Before I ever let you put on a pair of gloves, I told you that boxing was about *endurance*. Seeing your fight through to the end no matter how exhausted or defeated you are. Quitting is the worst thing a fighter can do. You only quit when you absolutely have to. Now, do you absolutely have to quit?"

"Dad, I got kicked out—"

"No, you don't have to quit," he continued. "So keep

going. Help Melanie. Help the football team. You want them to have those warm-up suits, don't you? Then fight for it," he said, sounding as determined as an old cutman. "Make sure no one takes that away from them— including you."

Dad hadn't talked with that much encouragement since he taught me my first jab.

"What about you, Dad? What are you doing about getting a job?" He looked back at the TV. "Are you still fighting? Because from the looks of things, it seems like you gave up a long time ago."

He sighed. "It's different, honey. Adult stuff is hard to understand."

"I don't believe that anymore. And you did teach me early on about keeping yourself protected. You said if you leave one small opening, the fighter will take advantage of that. I think that's what you did at work. Someone saw the opening you left and took advantage." He seemed to consider this, and if I say so myself, I thought it was a pretty darn good analogy. "You still don't have to throw in the towel."

He leaned over and patted my leg. "Smart girl," he said. "I'll get back in there if you will."

I smiled a great big smile at my dad like I hadn't

smiled at him in months. "Deal," I said, then jumped up from the couch.

"Where are you going?"

"Back to the fight!" I said as I hurried back to my room and shut my door.

As I sat down at my computer, I realized there were times when you should protect yourself, like I had just said to Dad, and times you shouldn't. I realized that with all of Melanie's jokes, with all her hobbies and flirting and outward happiness, she was just keeping herself protected too, from what had happened long ago with her mom. Maybe she was protecting herself from dealing with it. And even though it's good to keep yourself protected in the ring, it's not always good to do it in life.

So I sat down at the computer and wrote an e-mail:

Melanie:

First, I want to say I never got to thank you for being the first one to come to me about our fight. I was angry and I guess I was just going to let it end like that, but you made the first move. It was really brave of you, and I'm sorry I wasn't nicer about it.

Everything aside, the football team really

needs those warm-up suits. Mel, you can't quit now. They need you more now than they ever needed me.

I have an idea that I think will work, and it's really low-key—no one has to know, if you don't want them to. Whatever happened to us, especially about Cooper, I think this is important, and I think you do too.

If you're interested in this proposal, please sit next to me on the bus in the morning, or at least drop a note on my seat as you pass and we'll talk later in private.

Respectfully,

Lucia

★★★★★ 26 ★★★★★

The next day I went to Cooper's in the cold, dark morning air, obsessing over the e-mail. I knew the boxing would help me push out all that anxiety.

I took Cooper's blue hand wraps from him so I could do his hands. But he took them back and said, "No, I can do it."

"Since when?" I asked.

"Since now. I've been practicing. 'Bout time I learned to do it myself."

I watched him work the fabric around his wrists and knuckles and awkwardly between his fingers. When he was done, it was a little lumpy, and even though I worried he hadn't padded his knuckles enough, I told him it looked great.

We boxed hard, both of us, but there were no cheap

shots or breaking the rules. When we were done, we touched gloves and said, "Good match."

After my generic-bran-flakes breakfast, I waited on the corner for the bus with butterflies in my stomach almost as fierce as the morning of my election speech.

I saw the bus coming down the street, and when I heard a distant front door slam, my stomach gave a lurch. I stepped up the stairs of the bus.

I sat in my usual seat and watched Melanie cross in front of the bus, wearing a pea-green flat-cap.

She climbed up the bus stairs, and as she turned down the aisle, my heart pounded. She paused at my seat. She didn't look at me but looked into her bag, which matched her hat, like she was digging for something, a note maybe. As the bus pulled away, she stopped searching and continued past me without a word.

The guys in the back of the bus gave a little cheer as she sat with them ("Pied Piper!" they called).

What was *that*? Had she paused in the aisle just to mess with me? It was like she was flexing some sort of power over me.

All through the day, I couldn't stop thinking about her. At lunch Coop and I sat together with Max, but none of us spoke. Max kept darting his eyes between Cooper and me, and I kept looking at Cooper to see if I could read anything on his face about Melanie. Finally, Cooper snapped, "Everybody quit looking at me!" That's when Max looked at me and kind of shrugged, and we went back to eating.

There were so many things I loved about Melanie— her sense of adventure, her willingness to try anything— and that openness was something I knew I didn't have. I'd been jealous of her for it. But she never stuck around for the fight. And instead of feeling sorry for her, I got angry. She had to follow through and finish what she started—and what I also had started. *That*, I decided, showed responsibility. That showed true heart.

So, I cornered Melanie at her locker at the end of the day. The cutouts of the pies that were on her locker had been taken down. I hadn't heard too many people talking about P-Day since Nicole's article came out almost two weeks ago, and I had to wonder if Melanie herself was the one keeping the story alive.

"Hey," I said as she threw her books into her locker with what seemed like a little extra force. "Did you get my e-mail last night?" She sighed loudly, but I wasn't going to back down. "*Melanie,*" I said.

"Look, it's fine." She laughed, but it was totally fake. "You can do whatever you want for the football team, but I'll leave it to you. It's still really your gig anyway. I'm just the sub."

"Melanie, come on. Don't be like that."

"Like what?" she asked, a smile on her mouth but not in her eyes. "I just . . . thanks for wanting to include me and all, but you know I'd just screw it up."

"Stop it," I said. "Mel, I *need* your help. I can't do it alone." I softened my voice when I realized she was really listening to me. "Let's *not* quit together."

She seemed to consider this and stood scratching at the edge of her locker for a moment. "Are you trying to get back your presidency or something?"

"No," I said. "It's not like that at all. No one has to know I'm helping you. In fact, I don't want anyone to know. It'll be just between us."

The halls were quiet as most people had already headed out to the buses, which I started to worry we were going to miss. Again.

"Well, what's your brilliant plan?" she asked.

I smiled, relieved and excited about the project. "Easy. Divide and conquer."

★

Over the next week, we worked out a pretty simple plan. We became a two-person fund-raising machine. Only instead of asking the parents and students to donate to the football team, we asked the local businesses. Most of them had kids who either went to Angus or would one day. And even if they didn't, everyone loved watching Angus football to try to predict who would be the major players in high school, and even who had the potential to go pro.

I e-mailed Melanie a list of businesses we could easily hit, and we made plans on where to meet after school. And it turns out, we were a really good team. Melanie was great at charming the owners, and she always seemed to know just when to give me my moment to step in with the kill, the Big Ask. By the time we left, we almost always had a check.

After our last stop, we counted up the money.

"It's not enough," I said. I had already counted it three times.

"Are you sure?" Melanie asked.

"Positive."

We were at her house after our final round of hitting businesses. Most places had been really nice, and even with the deficit Melanie had created with the pie toss, I still couldn't believe it wasn't enough.

We were in the kitchen, which had more empty take-out boxes than dishes. During the time we'd spent together, doing our fund-raising shtick, I felt like I'd gotten to know another side of Melanie. She was outgoing, yes, but she was also really good at selling our cause, of telling everyone how important this was for our football team and school. She had a lot of passion in her that I hadn't realized before.

"Now what are we going to do?" I sighed. We'd exhausted every place in town, from the tiny mom-and-pop places to the big chain stores. My plan hadn't been good enough.

Melanie sighed, taking off her magic red beret and setting it on the table in front of us. "So much for magic, huh?"

The last time I'd seen her without a hat on had been when it got knocked off in the pie toss. Looking at her now, I saw that the dark brown of her hair made her brown eyes look even lighter, sort of translucent. Even though she looked adorable in her hats, I couldn't help but think they covered her up a little too much.

"What made you decide that hat was magic, any-way?" I asked.

"Mom gave it to me. Anytime she and Dad took a trip, she'd bring Beverly back a scarf and me a hat. It was like our thing. All the hats she gave me are way too small now, except this one. It's fit me since fourth grade." I knew that was the year her mom died, but didn't say anything. "Pretty dumb, huh?"

"Not at all. I think it's cool you have something from your mom that's special."

She nodded. "I miss her."

"I know," was all I said back. It didn't feel right to try to comfort her with words—I knew nothing about los-ing a parent.

We were quiet for what seemed like forever—a min-ute, maybe twenty. Finally, she began gathering up all the checks and money, and I said I better head home, start thinking of a new plan.

At the front door, she asked, "You still boxing with Cooper?"

"Yeah."

"I didn't mean to take it away from you when I tried it with him. It's just that, I've never known anyone, let alone a girl, who boxed. It's one of the coolest things about you."

"You can still try it, you know," I said. "I didn't mean, during all that, that you couldn't box if you wanted to."

"Just not with your gear, right?" She smiled, and I knew she was playing around.

"Hey, a girl's gear is a sacred thing. Like wearing someone else's magic hat."

"Right." Things seemed like they might go back to normal for us, but we were taking it slow. I couldn't believe I had ever thought, even for a brief moment, that she might vote for my impeachment. Sometimes I really was dumb, especially when it came to my friends.

Then suddenly, Melanie snapped her fingers and her face lit up—more so since she wasn't hidden by a hat. "I got it!" When I asked her what, she said, "A way to raise the extra money. The only thing is, you have to do it yourself."

Instead of being suspicious or rolling my eyes and asking why I had to do everything alone, I stepped back inside her house and listened to her plan.

27

"Keep your hands on either side of your face. Remember, you have to protect yourself! Jared, turn your hand flat when you hit. Rotate it. There! That's good!"

I walked around the school's gym and watched my fellow classmates learn the basics of boxing, all for the admission price of five bucks a person. Melanie convinced me to hold a one-hour boxing clinic. I'd had a similar idea months ago but was too chicken to go through with it. "Everyone's heard that you box, but people either don't believe it or want to know more," she'd told me.

"Why hasn't anyone ever asked?"

"Guess they were afraid to."

The idea for the workshop was totally different, unlike anything we'd ever done. We had advanced sign-up sheets so we could determine how much money we were going to make (no surprises, thank you very much). Ms. Jenkins noted that it was a great way to get the kids exercising in a new, fun way (although Mrs. Peoria grumbled something about violence begetting violence). And, most important, it was something everyone was excited about. They wanted to participate, and not just because they felt obligated to donate to the fundraiser. For once, everyone thought this sounded like a lot of fun. And I had Melanie to thank for that.

We had about fifty students sign up, so we brought in the coaches to help us out. But it wasn't the coaches who made it so special and worth the price of admission. One of the selling points of the workshop was having a trained professional there. I just had to convince said professional to do it.

I had gone to Dad one night after Melanie and I had agreed that we needed an expert there to help us, not just me showing what I knew about jabs and uppercuts.

I explained our idea to Dad and why we needed him. I knew about having good people on your team, helping you out and making you stronger. That shows real strength of character. "You taught me a lot about boxing," I told him. "But this can't possibly work without you."

"It's been a long time," Dad said.

"I know. That's why you should do it." He seemed to be thinking about it. "Dad, I'm asking for your help."

He looked at me, finally understanding. "Tell me when and where," he said.

After he agreed, I asked him if he could go to the old gym and see if they'd loan us some gloves and extra practice mitts. "I bet they'd be glad to see you," I said.

"Light on your feet, girl!" Dad called to April DeHart in the school gym. "Get on the balls of your feet. No, not like you're going to tiptoe! It's more subtle than that."

Dad demonstrated to the group he was working with. He told everyone to put their hands on the sides of their faces, then showed them how to shuffle back and forth. "It's the boxer shuffle," he said as his group—which also included Lily Schmidt, Cooper, and Melanie—bounced back and forth. "Good! Keep those hands up!"

Everyone had pulled through on the event—the whole student council, the coaches, and even some of the teachers. Nicole was there to cover it as a reporter, but it looked like she was having a great time, throwing punches into the mitts of Coach Ryan. Lori Anne took a bunch of photos but couldn't resist joining in, so she'd set her camera aside for some lessons too.

Dad circulated through the gym, checking everyone's form and making sure that the coaches were showing proper technique too. He looked more awake than I'd seen him in months.

The smacking of gloves on mitts filled the gym. "I want to hear that thunder!" Dad yelled.

BLUE JAYS . . .
THE VIEW FROM ABOVE
O'Hare's Secret Weapon
BY NICOLE JEFFRIES

Student council president Melanie O'Hare ends the calendar year on a high note with her presentation of the football team's much-needed warm-up suits. Approximately 75 students showed up before school, when Ms. O'Hare, along with Mrs. Peoria, built a fire in a trash can to help keep students warm, and mark the significance of the event.

"Even if hell freezes over and this team goes to state," Coach Fleck began, referring to one local news station's opinion of our fighting Blue Jays going all the way this year, "at least our boys will be warm enough to fight the devil!"

One person who was noticeably absent from the proceedings? Ousted president Lucia Latham, whose resignation marked the first time in Angus's history that such a scandal has ever happened.

Many wondered how Ms. O'Hare, more known for her hats than her work ethic, could have raised this money on her own.

"Of course I had help," Ms. O'Hare stated, her fuzzy cream-colored winter cap looking thirsty for a snowflake or two. "A good president always keeps herself surrounded with smart, hard-working people. I'm no different."

But this reporter learned, in fact, that it was Ms. Latham herself who worked in tandem with Ms. O'Hare to realize the success of the fund-raiser. The former foes were spotted traipsing in and out of local businesses in a joint effort to raise money for the football team.

In fact, it is believed that, without the help of the former president, the football team would still be left in the cold. It is no secret that William Latham, the former Golden Gloves junior middleweight champion who led the boxing clinic, is father to Ms. Latham. This clinic helped the eighth-grade class raise the money for the football team and pay back the difference lost in Ms. O'Hare's ill-fated Pie Toss.

Here's to Ms. O'Hare, who took a hard hit but kept on fighting. She's a true Blue Jay through and through.

★★★★★ 28 ★★★★★

I didn't go to the big check- and plaque-presenting ceremony. It was held outside near the coaches' temporary offices in the cold before school. Mrs. Peoria had made exactly one decision so far this year with the student council, and that was it.

You'd be surprised at how okay people were with getting to school an hour early and standing in the freezing cold. The ceremony was tradition, and the fact that the student council raised money for the football team made it even huger, because who doesn't want to support their football team? The very best part, though, was that this year's student council raised more money than any other council, ever.

But like I said, I didn't go.

I didn't *not* go on purpose. Well, okay, maybe I did a little bit. But also I didn't know I was going to get woken up by Dad at six o'clock that morning.

"Come on, girl," he whispered in the dark. "Get your gear and meet me in the kitchen."

It all felt so covert—the dark early morning, the whispering and tiptoeing—that I was out of bed before Dad had even left my room. Plus, I smelled bacon frying.

In the kitchen, Dad flipped what I instantly recognized as his classic whole-wheat pancakes. In another pan, the bacon fried.

"What is all this?" I asked, but quietly. Despite the noise of the bacon, the house was so still that I didn't want to break any spells.

"You'll need your energy," Dad said as he stacked my plate with two pancakes and slices of bacon. He set a glass of orange juice beside my plate.

I looked at the carton. "The real stuff?"

"Mom couldn't stand the cheap stuff anymore." He winked at me as I poured syrup on my pancakes, making sure to drizzle a bit on the bacon as well.

After we ate, I was so excited to realize that Dad was driving us to his old gym. When we walked inside, it was as if we had entered a different time zone. The gym was completely alive and awake with stomping, pounding, buzzing energy. Guys, and a couple of girls, were jumping rope, hitting bags, and sparring in each of the two rings. I let myself get filled up with the energy.

Dad walked easily across the gym, a couple of guys calling out his name as he went.

"Back again? You gonna make this regular?" a slim, cute guy asked Dad.

When we got to the side of the gym, Dad told me to get my wraps on. Being in the gym was exhilarating but intimidating. The people there were serious—it was no hobby for them.

Once my hands were wrapped, I said to Dad, "Don't you dare ask me to get in that ring. No way am I ready for that."

"Your momma would have my head if I tried that," he said. "I'm going to teach you what I should have taught you last summer. The speedbag."

There was a special bag that was lower than the others I could just reach it. As Dad showed me how to hit the bag ("Count, shift your feet slightly, and don't forget—it's not really about speed"), I realized that this was in my dad's blood, which meant that it was in mine as well.

I was glad I was at the gym instead of the ceremony. Melanie deserved to have the spotlight all to herself.

She'd implemented the whole thing—I'd just brought Dad in. She and I had both learned an important lesson: The key to success is about surrounding yourself with people who complement you, who make your best even better. And we were both surprised to find out we were a pretty good team. I had learned that everyone works differently, and I don't have all the answers or the best work ethic, necessarily.

By the time I got to school, the ceremony was over. Ms. Jenkins actually let the football guys wear their warm-up suits to school that day, so the halls were extra festive, as if it were a game day.

"Hey, Coop!" I called when I saw him walking down the halls. "So how'd it go this morning?"

"It was great!" Cooper said. "You should have come. I missed you. Where were you?"

"With my dad, boxing."

"What, I'm not good enough for you anymore?" He lightly punched my arm.

"Please. You're my best sparring partner ever," I said, punching him back.

"Are you upset about not getting your name on that plaque?"

Mike Tyson once said that everybody has a plan

until they get punched in the mouth. I was finally starting to realize that. Planning was good—expecting the unexpected and knowing your opponent backward and forward was important. You had to approach things the smart way. Just like Ray Arcel, a legendary boxing trainer, once said, "Boxing is brain over brawn," and that's how I wanted to live my life. Even though you can't control how things will turn out, when you're hit with a dilemma, you have a choice in how you handle it. I hadn't made all the right choices this year—like not telling what I knew to be the truth about the research period and scheduled voting—and I'd lost a lot of trust and respect from my peers because of that. But I'd work hard to earn it all back. Boxing was about respect, and so was life.

"Not at all," I told Cooper. "In fact, I'm glad everything happened the way it did."

"Seriously?" When I told him I was, he said, "Well, I hope so. Because the school year is only half over."

I moaned when I realized that. But you know what? It was still a great year. I fought hard, and I learned that I could take a hit and keep going. And I'd *never* let myself get knocked down again.